Dusty Dreams

Sherri Ward

DUSTY DREAMS

SHERRI WARD

ISBN-10: 0692781307
ISBN-13: 978-0692781302

Butterfly Feet Publishing

Fort Collins, Colorado, USA
butterflyfeetpublications.com

CHAPTER ONE

"I've carried your brother far enough, Jen." Jerome hesitated before adding, "You were never going to marry me anyway." His eyes watched Jennifer keenly, searching her face for any sign he could be wrong.

Jennifer stared speechlessly for a moment at the man she'd known since childhood. "Jer, I never said I would marry you. You never said that was part of the bargain."

Jerome looked down, scuffing at the dusty ground with his boot before lifting his chin resolutely. "I'm moving on. I have to. You and Russell will have to make the best of things until the next wagon train comes through. If you don't want to wait for it, you can go back to that town we passed a ways back."

Jennifer felt a sense of near panic as she looked around at their desolate surroundings. Bleakly watching Jerome walk back to his own wagon, she batted away a fly and wiped the sweat off the back of her neck. *Is he really and truly going to abandon us here? How could he? "I'll marry you!" That's all I have to say.* She continued to stare wordlessly as the small train of wagons flanked by a few men on horseback rolled and creaked away.

"Lord, what are we going to do?" she whispered. Brushing the dust off her long skirts, she climbed up into the wagon she had shared with her brother for the last two months. Although the air inside the wagon was oppressively hot, she felt at least she could tolerate it more easily than the blistering heat of the direct sunlight.

As she sat on a chest in the wagon, a sense of utter isolation nearly overwhelmed her. Taking a deep breath, she silently scolded herself. *Russell will return soon; don't be so gloomy! It's not as bad as all that – is it, Lord? Besides, Mother would remind me that I'm never really alone because You are always with me.* Her attempts at bravery didn't seem to do much to chase her feelings of despair away. "I wish Mother were here," she whispered aloud as a tear ran down her dusty cheek.

She thought back on how they happened to be in this predicament. Their parents had both passed away, and with no other close relatives in New England, the chance to claim land and a new life in the west had been a captivating notion even for Jennifer, and her brother Russell had eagerly jumped at the opportunity. She remembered his excitement when he had told her that Jerome had agreed to let them go along even though they had little money. He had become more serious though when he had said, "Jen, I need to tell you something. Jerome thinks there's a chance you'll marry him."

"Oh Russ, no! Surely you didn't tell him I'd do any such thing!" she had exclaimed in alarm.

His reply had been quick. "No, of course I didn't say you would! I told him flat out it was very unlikely and that he

2

shouldn't count on it." He remained still for a moment and then he quietly added, "I just think he hopes you'll change your mind, that's all."

Quite sure marrying Jerome was something she would never change her mind about, Jennifer had turned her thoughts to what life might be like out west. "Well, if we can go along that'll be great. We can't afford land here, but maybe out West we can have our own real place, maybe with a nearby stream, and a nice log cabin." She had sighed dreamily. "Won't it be great? We can find some land near a settlement, and maybe do some farming or even ranching, and maybe eventually I can even teach school!"

They had worked hard over the next few weeks to settle their affairs in preparation for the trip. The house they had grown up in was sold, along with almost everything in it. Although it was heart wrenching for Jennifer to watch the furnishings and household goods of their childhood home being sold at auction, it was the only thing to do. They needed money to buy a wagon and the horses to haul it as well as supplies for the long trip.

It was also difficult to leave behind the friends they held dear. In particular Jennifer remembered wistfully the day she had said goodbye to her lifelong and best friend in the world, Caroline. They had both cried and promised to write. As she thought about her now though, she couldn't help but wonder if she would ever even see her again.

At last all of their plans to join with the wagon train had worked out as they had hoped, and they had set out on the trail with Jerome and a few other bold adventurers, most of whom had paid a sizeable sum of money for the opportunity to be guided west and protected by Jerome and his hired guns.

At first thrilled beyond anything she had ever experienced, Jennifer's sense of adventure had faded to a weary disenchantment over the following weeks as the cool and lush green of the east had given way to the parched and dusty plains of the west.

Despondent, she sat now inside the wagon and stared out through the opening in the canvas cover. She could see their one remaining horse tethered by the little creek in the sparse shade of a small tree. Another tear trickled down her cheek as she remembered the disaster of earlier that day. The other horse had had the misfortune of stepping into a large cavity left by a burrowing varmint, and had been shot due to the resulting broken leg.

At last she heard Russell whistling a tune as he approached. *Whistling! Surely he sees that all the other wagons have departed! Will he even now insist on being cheerful?* She climbed out of the wagon and sighed in exasperation as he smiled happily and held up the day's catch, a couple of trout. Ignoring the fish, she exclaimed, "Russell, what are we going to do? Jerome has left us! He has abandoned us here all alone on the prairie!"

Russell stopped grinning and put the fish on a nearby rock. "I know, Jennifer. He told me this morning they'd be moving on before I went off to have a look around and do a little fishing." He leaned toward her and ventured a quick kiss on her forehead in spite of her hands planted resolutely on her hips and the glare that admonished his carefree attitude.

Later that evening the two of them sat near the creek, having eaten the fish they had cooked over the open fire along with a few biscuits.

"Russell, what are we going to do? In case you haven't noticed, we are in the middle of nowhere!" Although she was aware that the question weighed heavily on him already and that nagging wouldn't help, it seemed impossible to keep silent when everything was going so wrong. Besides, she hadn't said anything about it for nearly an hour, and felt that because she had held her tongue for so long perhaps it was time to try again to start the conversation they surely had to have.

Deep in thought, Russell waited a moment before replying. "Jen, there's something I want to show you. Tomorrow we're going to take a ride. We'll saddle up the horse and just go for a short ride. Okay?"

She didn't answer for a moment, then blurted out, "Russell, we could just turn around now and go back home. We don't have to keep going on, we could just go back instead." When he didn't answer, she added, "All this stuff that's happened, it's not our fault. It's not our fault it's been such a long, tough journey. It's not our fault the horse got his leg broke. It's not our fault Jerome went on without us." Russell didn't answer, so she pressed on desperately, trying to think of anything to say that might make him consider the situation realistically. "It's not our fault it's so desolate out here on the prairie, and life is hard, and there's nothing here to make it any better! Our friends are all back east, and all of the stores are back east, and, well, just everything. Everything is back east." Her voice trailed off. *What else can I say? Lord, why won't he be reasonable?*

Russell stopped staring into the fire and, smiling slightly, cocked his head at her as if to see if she were finished. Then he sighed and said quietly, "I know all these things, Jen. And I'm sorry it's been so hard. But it's not over. I need you to stay tough for a while longer." He paused and stirred up the fire before saying, "The thing is, going back is simply not an option any more. Even if we still had both horses, going back would be an even tougher journey and more dangerous than it has been getting here. We had the help of Jerome and his men and the other wagons getting this far, but if we turned back we'd be on our own. And the fact also is that we don't have both horses, so we can't pull the wagon." Neither said anything for several moments, and then he said, "I want to show you something. Tomorrow."

Jennifer sighed, but said resignedly, "Okay." How showing her anything out here in this remote and barren land would help she had no idea, but she decided not to think about it.

Dejectedly, she got up and set about cleaning up the few dishes in the creek. As she worked, she thought about how much Russell was like their mother. Like her, nothing ever seemed to make him panic, and his faith in God never seemed to waver. Jennifer envied that faith in him at times, although at other times she felt he just might be somewhat over the top with it all. Now here they were, and while he remained calm and unshaken in spite of their predicament, she found herself questioning whether, in fact, God Himself really even existed, at least in the way she had always been told He did.

She thought back on the times her mother had read to them from the scriptures, and how important church had been to her and in their lives. It seemed nothing short of a blizzard ever kept them all from getting to church on a Sunday morning. Even if you were ill, you practically had to be on your death bed before she would hear of you staying home from church. The memories Jennifer really treasured though, were walks and talks when her mother would talk about God almost as if He were right there with them. She loved pointing out flowers and birds and all the wonder of His creation.

It was the closeness of the church fellowship that had gotten them through the most difficult time surrounding their father's death, and again with the passing of their mother. If they could somehow even now choose to go back, she knew the church would welcome them with open arms. She truly missed the laughter and sharing of secrets among some of the girls her own age, especially Caroline.

She couldn't help but wonder where God was at this moment. If He did exist, perhaps He was ignoring their plight because He was angry at them for making the journey in the first place. There was no church out here on the desolate prairie that she knew of. And they hadn't actually heard a majestic voice telling them to buy horses and a wagon and head west to some unknown destination. Well, it was too late to think about that now. They were here, and they had no choice but to make the best of things. She hurried to finish cleaning up so she could spend some time relaxing by the fire before they rolled out the sleeping blankets for the night.

She awoke the next morning to the smell of coffee and flapjacks. Remembering Russell's plan to go for a ride, she hurried to change into a pair of riding pants and an old shirt before exiting the wagon and helping herself to coffee. Before long breakfast was done and they were both mounted on the horse and making their way alongside the creek. Russell had continued to keep the destination secret, saying only, "You'll see soon enough." True to his word, within a fairly short time they were riding up a slope, and at the top of the hill Jennifer drew in her breath in wonder. The view was one of a stunningly beautiful river valley extending as far north as the eye could see.

"Isn't it beautiful, Jennifer? The creek we're camped at is

only a tributary. Look at that river! Look at the valley and how green it is! Look at all the trees, and water – see, there's a lake over there. Look, it's a forest of trees, and more hills, and look at the mountain peaks to the west – they even have snow on top!"

Jennifer could only stare in speechless amazement.

Later that evening as they sat by the fire, Jennifer couldn't help but feel that Russell was brooding about something. They had talked about what they had seen that day, and Russell had shared his thoughts and feelings. Just knowing the river and valley and mountains were there had given him hope that it was completely possible to live off the land. "I can fish and trap and we can grow a lot of our own food, maybe even raise some livestock. And there is that town nearby, so we could always get supplies. Jennifer, I believe if God is willing this might very well be a good place for us."

Jennifer herself had begun to have hope, and had voiced no disagreement, so she couldn't help but wonder, now that the conversation had dwindled, why he still seemed to be troubled about something. It occurred to her that perhaps he still somehow felt bad that they were in this situation and that he was blaming himself, or maybe he even felt that she blamed him. After a while of neither speaking, she finally said quietly, "Russ, you know I don't blame you."

"Hmm?"

"You know, for bringing us out here in the first place. We both wanted to come out here, I was nearly as excited about it as you. And it's not your fault. All this stuff that's happened."

"Russell sighed and turned his gaze back to the fire. "Jen, you know I love you and I promised Mom I'd take good care of you. So I am responsible for our being here. Still, Dad used to say that that nothing good ever comes about without some trouble along the way. I just hope and pray…" His voice trailed off, but as Jennifer started to ask what he was thinking, he said, "Nothing, it's nothing. We just have a ways to go before we're surviving well out here, that's all."

Jennifer thought for another moment and then said, "Russell, Mom and Dad would be very proud of you. I'm not exactly sure what they might say about all this, or about our coming out here to begin with. But I think maybe they would not have been against it. And I just know they would be very proud of you."

The following morning, Jennifer rummaged through one of the chests in the wagon and found a few things – her Bible, a sheaf of letter writing stationery, and a small bound journal she used as a diary. She also found some blank paper for sketching along with pens and pencils. After climbing out of the wagon, she sat on a small wooden crate in the wagon's shade. Nearby the morning's fire had died out completely. More coffee sounded good, but she wasn't about to start another fire just to have some. Besides, they were on their last can of coffee and she didn't know just how long it would be before they got to a store or trading post. She took a sip from her water flask and dutifully opened her Bible as she did most days. "Seek the Lord every morning, seek Him early," her mother had always said. "He'll give you strength for the day."

After reading a bit, and saying a few short prayers, she set the Bible aside and picked up the sheaf of paper. *I should work on my letter to Caroline, but I don't really know when I will be able to mail it. Besides if I write to her I will have to mention the dead horse. And that buzzards are beginning to circle. If Caroline knew all that's happened, will she tell others? Will they think we have failed? Well, why would it matter? At least they would know we tried. And why is it that writing in my diary always seems easier than writing a letter? Oh well. Maybe I will do that later today or even tomorrow. Not like there's a lot to do around here anyway!* With a dismissive shrug, she put down the stationery and picked up the diary instead.

'Dear diary,' she wrote, 'Although we are still out here in the very middle of nowhere, the beautiful view we saw yesterday of a river and lakes and forests and even mountains gives us hope. And there is that town we passed only perhaps a couple of days back, so I guess I have to admit that it isn't truly completely desolate here.' She thought for a moment, and then wrote, 'I saw a cute little bird this morning, one I have never seen before. It was rather small and grayish brown, maybe like a sparrow, but it made the prettiest song notes I have not heard before. I would love to know what it is. Someday I shall buy a book and learn all about birds. I don't think I want to know so much about the buzzards, on the other hand. That poor horse has been dead only a couple of days, and already those big black things are circling. It's all so very gruesome!'

Suddenly she heard a noise and stopped writing. Russell hadn't been gone that long so she would be surprised if he were already back. She sat still, listening until she heard it again – the unmistakable clip-clop of a horse's hooves. It wasn't his habit to approach so slowly, but who else could it be? Likely he had forgotten something he wanted to take along. She rose to greet him, smiling as she walked around the wagon. The smile vanished and her heart skipped a beat as she beheld, not her brother as she expected, but an Indian man mounted on a horse.

The man reigned in his horse and stared at her, for a moment appearing nearly as startled as she felt. He quickly regained his composure, however, and without speaking began a slow, inquisitive circle around Jennifer and the wagon, stopping briefly to peer inside the wagon. After he had made a complete circle he stopped again in front of her. "You, woman, alone?"

"No, I'm not alone, my brother, I'm here with my brother," Jennifer stammered nervously.

The Indian made another slow, sharp-eyed pass around the wagon, this time looking more carefully into the wagon and all around the campsite.

"You shoot horse?" He waved an arm toward the unfortunate casualty of two days ago.

"No, the men – I don't know which one – the men of the wagon train, they had to shoot the horse. He broke his leg." Jennifer glanced at the dead horse with flies buzzing all over it and buzzards circling overhead.

The Indian rode around again slowly, this time examining the dusty ground with all the imprints left by wagons and horses. "You, woman, all alone. Brother leave you here."

Jennifer wanted to cry. "No, my brother will be right back! He said he would, he said he'd be home soon." Her voice trailed off as she stared at the man uneasily.

The man stared back at her inquisitively and then moved to the shady side of the wagon. Pointing at her Bible on the wooden crate, he asked, "You read? You know Jesus?" Watching her carefully, he slowly dismounted from his horse.

"Yes, I read," she said hesitantly. "I know Jesus."

"You read now. I listen. I wait. Brother come back soon." Slowly, the man seated himself on the ground in the shade and motioned for Jennifer to sit on the crate.

After staring at him uncertainly for a moment, Jennifer picked up the Bible and sat down. Clearing her throat, she opened it to the Psalms, and after another hesitant glance at her visitor, she found the 23rd Psalm and began to read in a quiet and nervous voice. "The Lord is my shepherd, I shall not want..."

As she read, in spite of her discomfiting circumstance, she remembered the words of her mother, "Stepping out in faith can be almost fun, in a way – rather like Jesus when he walked on water. But learning to stand in faith is what really gets you through the hard times." *God, are You here with me? I really need you right now!*

As she finished the psalm, she glanced again at the man, who was calmly nodding his approval. "Good, good. You read more."

CHAPTER TWO

Jennifer looked at Russell's solemn face and laughed lightheartedly as they sat that evening in front of the fire. They had finished eating the simple meal she had prepared from their meager provisions, and they were now reflecting on the day. "Russ, why are you so solemn?" she scolded her brother affectionately. "We have made a friend way out here on the prairie wilderness!"

"It could have gone the other way," Russell replied seriously. "He could have been a man looking for trouble. He might have hurt you. It was dumb for me to go off and leave you alone here. Maybe the dumbest thing I have ever done!" He sighed in exasperation at himself. "Besides, if I had stayed here, I would have been here when he showed up, and the answer to our problem would right now be the same as it is."

Jennifer shook her head and smiled as she thought about how uncharacteristically they were both behaving at the moment. Normally he scoffed at danger and she cringed at the mere thought of any bad thing happening. "You did what we both felt you had to do. We had no way of knowing a friendly, helpful Indian would come along and solve our problem for us."

Russell sighed with reluctant agreement.

"Besides," Jennifer went on with a giggle, "I can't think when I have ever read so much of the scriptures at one sitting. And I can't say I have ever prayed so much in one day, either!" She laughed again in delight and amazement as she thought back over the day.

The Indian had stayed and she had read from her Bible until Russell showed up early in the afternoon. After his initial shock at seeing an Indian sitting with his sister had passed, the two men had become acquainted, walking down to the creek while they talked.

Jennifer had stayed by the wagon, sketching absent-mindedly on her paper while pretending not to overhear what they were saying. Russell was explaining how they happened to be abandoned on the desolate plain. The Indian had a simple solution – he would go back to his people, and the next day he would return with a harness-trained horse to replace the dead one. When Russell had explained they didn't have much to offer in trade, the Indian had waved his arm graciously and said that anything would be enough. When Russell had still hesitated, the man had lifted his chin stubbornly and admitted a bit defiantly, "My people stole horse from your people! Now horse for anything is good trade!" Russell had nodded in wary understanding.

Now he stared at the fire in subdued silence. Finally he said, "The truth is, when I left today I had in mind to try to find his people. Jerome had told me before they left that there was a friendly tribe in these parts. He said they remain on good terms with the nearby town mostly because they trade with them. There are occasional skirmishes, but nothing too serious."

Jennifer replied, "Then I don't understand what you're so glum about! We have found them, or they, it seems, have found us, and they are being friendly and helpful. "

"One of them is being friendly. You know, Jennifer, we can't exactly count on everyone we happen to meet being as welcoming as this man, Indian or otherwise."

"Well, just as you always say, we'll have to deal with things as they come along. Right?" When he didn't answer, she added, "You're always telling me worrying over what might happen never helps, and that I should just believe God will take care of us just as He says He will. We couldn't move on from here without another horse to pull the wagon; I just don't know what we would have done! Russell, God has answered our prayers!"

Russell sighed. Then with a weak smile he said, "I know, little sister, you are right. I think I just shouldn't leave you out here alone any more no matter what." He stood up and tossed another log onto the fire, sending a few glowing sparks up into the inky blackness of the night. Then he said, "Tomorrow if the man comes back with a horse as he said, that will be great. We can hitch up the team and go to that town. We need supplies, and maybe we can find a place to stay there for now, and hopefully I can find someone who will have some work for me so we can make some money."

Although Jennifer nodded and said simply, "Okay," she couldn't help but think there was something more on his mind than he was willing to talk about, something that made him uneasy. But she hadn't gotten him to talk about it the night before, and it was obvious she would get nothing more about it from him now, so she dropped the subject and turned her thoughts to the trip they planned to make the next day. They hadn't stopped at a town in a few weeks, and the possibility of a hotel room with a hot bath for the night sounded heavenly. She was distracted from her thoughts by the sound of coyotes howling in the distance. Shivering, she pulled her shawl tightly around her shoulders.

Noticing her reaction to the coyotes' howls, Russell laughed. "Don't worry Sis, they won't come near the fire!"

She sniffed at him. "Says you!" *At least he's laughing at something, better than to keep on brooding!*

Jennifer shifted uncomfortably on the hard wooden plank seat of the wagon and searched a pocket to find a handkerchief to dab away the sweat from her brow and the back of her neck. *If this is what Russ had in mind when he said he'd not be leaving me alone any more, well, he'll just have to think again.* Of course, she wasn't exactly alone now that they had finally arrived in the small town of Wolcott. She smiled slightly and nodded at two women who were walking together on the boardwalk in front of the general store. They nodded back without smiling, and even seemed to be staring at her somewhat disapprovingly. Perhaps it was the tired horses melting in the afternoon sun they frowned on, but she felt it more likely to be her own rumpled and sweaty appearance that stirred their displeasure.

As they entered the store she shrugged indifferently as she looked up and down at their tidy dresses and sunbonnets. "Lord," she whispered, "They look just like they stepped off 6th Avenue in Boston. Whatever are they doin' in this tiny stick of a town way out here in the middle of this prairie desert?" She brushed the dust off her own dress a bit and tried to adjust the strands of hair falling out from under her sunbonnet. *They'd look a little rumpled and sweaty too if they'd had to travel by wagon and even do some walking in the hot sun through the prairie desert just to get to this little town!*

She thought back over the events of the morning. She and Russell had been relieved when their new friend the Indian, true to his word, had shown up leading a harness-trained horse. The trading was nothing more involved than a bit of friendly bickering. "No, no, too much, too much!" the man had insisted, and in the end Russell had settled for giving up a few of their mother's trinkets and a very small amount of cash for the horse they desperately needed. They both felt forever in the man's debt.

Their intention was to go east, retracing the route they had taken west with the wagon train until they reached the point where they remembered Jerome had pointed out the town from a distance. However, the Indian had disagreed. "No, no, too far! Too much trouble, it take maybe two long days." Finding a twig, he had stooped down and drawn a simple map in the dirt. Apparently Jerome had taken a large detour around the town to avoid it, something Jennifer at least found perplexing.

The man talked as he pointed to his scribbled dirt map. "You stay on road, like this, and you get to this fork in road. You turn here. Now you go straight into town, no trouble, it not take so long. Half day maybe."

Russell nodded. He had seen the fork in the road on his ventures to scout the area, but had ridden on it only a short distance before turning back. Although he'd been curious as to where the road led, he hadn't wanted to leave Jennifer alone any longer that day, and so he had returned to camp.

Convinced to take the road as the man had said, they had quickly finished getting their camp broken down and everything into the wagon. Then, after getting the horses harnessed, they had set out. To make sure they didn't get lost, the man even rode with them, departing only when the town had finally come into view.

Although it had been hot, Jennifer had walked a good part of the way to avoid being bounced and tossed on the hard seat of the wagon. While she walked, she wondered why Jerome had gone to such lengths not to go near the town. Towns were usually a welcome sight because they provided supplies and baths and other things needed by weary travelers. She also wondered about some of the hushed conversation between Russell and the Indian, and why Russell still seemed to be troubled about something. She had told herself that it wouldn't help to fret, and maybe it was nothing serious anyway. She also thought that once they got to the town and were finally surrounded by some civilization again he would begin to feel better about things.

The town was small, and they had easily found the general store on the main street. Tying the horses to the hitching rail, they had gone inside to procure supplies. Then, after Russell had helped her get everything they had purchased into the wagon, he had said something about trying to find someone who might be able to give him a job, or at least a day or two of work, and he had gone to the saloon while she continued to shuffle things around inside the wagon trying to make the best use of the cramped storage space.

She knew the storage space wouldn't be so cramped if the wagon only held clothes and blankets, cooking pots, dishes and other such necessities. In particular, there was a large trunk which held mostly nonessential keepsakes she couldn't bring herself to part with because they reminded her of their parents and the life they once shared. Included were some photographs, a couple of pretty vases, a few assorted pieces of fine china and a few other trinkets their mother had treasured.

While she had worked to organize and store the provisions, she had thought about opening the trunk. It wouldn't have been to add anything to it as it was already completely full. What she had really wanted was just to look at her mother's wedding dress that lay folded and wrapped neatly in paper in the bottom of the chest. Her mother had always said she could wear it for her own wedding day, but Jennifer couldn't help but think the dress might never be worn again. Still, it gave her comfort to caress the silky white fabric and lace while she dreamed of finding that one special man who would care for her forever. But she had told herself that Russell would be back any moment, and it wouldn't do to have the contents of the trunk strewn about, so she had left the trunk closed, finished arranging supplies the best she could, and climbed out onto the wagon seat to dutifully wait for him.

Now while she waited, she looked around again at the few buildings which lined the dirt road. One, she was sure, was the horse livery, and there was the blacksmith right next to it. A few of the buildings appeared to be small houses, and she couldn't help but wonder who might live in them. While she watched, two young boys ran down the street laughing and shouting, both batting at some sort of ball with sticks. A dog followed, apparently trying to play the game too by snatching the ball whenever he had a chance. The boys, however, would yell whenever he managed to snatch the ball, so he would drop it and wait for another chance. Shortly one of the boys picked the ball up and, taking the dog with them, they went inside one of the houses.

The sight stirred memories of her own childhood, and the pangs of nostalgia brought a few tears trickling down her dusty cheeks. Their mother had never minded too much when Jennifer dressed in boy clothes. That way her pretty dresses weren't torn or dirtied when she climbed the trees and fences with Russell and the neighborhood boys. Some of the other ladies in town had not approved, but her mother always felt it was important for children to get outside and run off some energy. *How wonderful it would be to be in our old backyard right now, and hear Mother calling us in for lemonade! That would taste so good in this heat!* But she knew it wasn't really so much about cold lemonade as it was that she missed her mother and the sheltering love she had raised them in.

Well, that can't be helped now, no sense thinking about it! Wiping off the tears, she sat up straighter and reluctantly allowed her gaze to go back to the saloon where she had last seen her brother. He had stood for a few moments, staring over the swinging half doors. Then he had looked back at her with a reassuring smile before pushing open one of the doors and going inside. She could still hear the rowdy laughter and piano music, but Russell had not reappeared.

As the time passed with still no sign of him, Jennifer began to feel more and more restless and concerned. *How long can it take to ask a few questions about the availability of work?* It wasn't that he never went into such a place, but he certainly wasn't the type to drink much, especially this early in the day, and never when there was so little money to live on. *Whatever can be taking him so long?* It had been such a long day already, and the late afternoon sun was baking everything including her. She sighed again and wiped more sweat off the back of her neck. She stared for a few moments again at the horses with their heads hung low and their tails constantly whisking away the flies. It simply was not like Russell to leave them in the sun so long if he could help it. Finally she could endure the wait no longer. After another apprehensive glance at the saloon, she determinedly stood up and climbed down from the wagon.

CHAPTER THREE

Jennifer walked slowly across the small dirt road which separated the saloon and the general store. As she stepped up onto the boardwalk, she realized she had never gone this close to the doors of a saloon before. She remembered her mother's warning, "Stay just as far away from those places as you can, Jen, they are no place for God-fearing women!" Jennifer hesitated as she stepped up onto the boardwalk. Then she sighed and whispered, "I'm sorry, Mom, but I just don't know what else to do! I'll take just a quick peek because I have to find Russ!" *If I can just see him, perhaps talking to someone, then I'll know he's okay and I'll go back to the wagon to wait some more. That's probably all it is, he's talking to someone about some work!*

By peering over the swinging doors she could make out through the dim light and cigar smoke that it was all pretty much like she thought it would be. In the corner, a lively man in a red and white striped shirt pounded out brassy tunes on a cheap piano. Several men stood at the bar with tall glasses of beer or short shots of whiskey in front of them. A couple of round tables were occupied by men playing poker. However, a quick scan of the entire room confirmed what she had feared – Russell was not there. She turned away quickly and hurried back toward the wagon.

Stopping near the boardwalk where the horses were tied to the hitching rail, she looked around the town again, letting her eyes come to rest on the door of the general store. She knew the women she had seen earlier could still be in there, and she didn't look forward to their disapproving stares. However, she wanted to talk to the store owner, and could think of nothing else to do, so she went inside. The women were at the counter paying for their purchases.

Jennifer wandered aimlessly toward the back of the store. When she and Russell had been in earlier, she had noticed some bolts of fabric and a sewing machine. There were also sewing novelties – spools of thread, cards of elastic and lace trimmings. She had stopped to lightly caress the fabric and to stare at the machine, thinking of all the pretty things she could sew. Russell had stopped looking through various supplies to caution her, "You know we can't afford any of that right now. Maybe someday soon, but not right now."

"I know, Russ," she had replied. "I'm just looking. Look at all this pretty fabric, and I love all the different colors of thread! And can you believe that machine? What an amazing invention it is!" She looked at the machine now without really seeing it, her mind reeling as to where Russell could possibly be.

The ladies were leaving the store, so Jennifer walked to the counter and spoke to the owner. "I hate to be a bother, but I just don't know what else to do."

"You're not a bother, Missy, how can I help you?" The man smiled graciously.

"My brother – he was in here with me earlier – he went into the saloon hoping to find someone to talk to about getting some work – but that was quite a while ago, and I haven't seen him since."

The store owner's good humor seemed to drain from his face and his smile was replaced with a frown. "That was quite a good while ago. You ain't seen him since?"

"No, and I did go over just now and peek inside the saloon, and he's not in there! It just isn't like him to leave the horses standing out in the sun all day like this." She wanted to add that he had promised not to leave her all alone any more either, but she felt that would take too much explanation, so instead she remained silent and waited for the store owner's reply.

The man let out a heavy sigh. "No, I don't suppose it is like him to leave the horses like that." Placing both hands on the counter he stared down at his feet for a moment, and then, without looking up, he cursed so quietly Jennifer almost didn't hear it. But she did hear it, and her apprehension grew.

God, where is my brother? What is going on that Russell didn't want to tell me? "Sir, I don't know exactly how to ask this, but is there something going on in this town, something that might cause a person to be concerned or troubled?"

The man suddenly stood up straight and scowled at her. "You young kids," he almost spat out the words, "You come out here looking for cheap land and easy visions. Well, there's nothin' cheap and there's nothin' easy out here, and you all oughta just get back in that wagon and go back east where you came from!"

Jennifer drew back in alarm at his intensity.

23

Shaking his head, the man went on, "Now look, I surely don't mean to frighten you, but those boys from the west end are in town today!"

"The West End?" Baffled, Jennifer could only stare at him as her fears mounted.

The man shook his head again in hopelessness at the frightened and bewildered look on Jennifer's face. "The west end of town! Now look, you and your brother seem like nice folks. Why'd ya have to pick this town to stop in? You're sure better off goin' back where you came from! Or even keep on moving west! This town is no place for..." Letting his voice trail off, the man shook his head and stared down at his feet again.

Jennifer realized that although he was not deliberately trying to frighten her, he was quite sincere in his efforts to convince her to take her brother and leave town immediately. *Lord, what could be so wrong in this town that would cause this man to act so strangely?* Standing as straight as she could and lifting her chin resolutely she replied as plainly as she could possibly speak, "Sir, even if I wanted to leave this town right now, I could not because I do not know where my brother is!"

Just then the sound of boots thudding on the boardwalk drew their attention to the doorway and store window. A man was outside on the boardwalk and he seemed to be snooping around the wagon. Jennifer watched in alarm as he peeked into the wagon while drawing a gun out of its holster. She took a step, intent on leaving the store and confronting him, but the store owner reached out quickly and grabbed her arm. "Missy, you stand fast!" he spoke quietly yet fiercely. "You do not want to go out there!"

Her instinct was to retract her arm, but he held it

unyieldingly, so she stifled the urge to cry out and instead looked at him questioningly.

"You must trust me!" He continued to speak almost in a whisper, both sternly and pleadingly. "There is a storage room through that doorway back there. Go quietly right now, and find a place to hide there. Hurry! Do not come out until I tell you it is safe, do you understand me?"

Any sense of peace that Jennifer might have felt at any time during this strange day was completely gone now. After a quick glance at the man out on the boardwalk with his gun drawn, she nodded briefly at the store owner and hurried to do exactly as he had said. Hastening to the storage room, she quickly found a place to hide behind a few large grain barrels. As she crouched down behind one, she couldn't help but notice the dust. It was obvious that most of the efforts to keep up a tidy appearance went into the front of the store. Ignoring the dust, she drew her skirts in tightly around herself so nothing would be visible.

Within a few moments she heard voices and knew that the man with the gun was now inside the store talking to the owner. She strained to hear what was being said but they spoke too quietly for her to make out more than a word or two. Then she heard footsteps approaching the back room slowly. Was it the store owner, coming to tell her all was clear? Not likely she decided, as certainly the store owner would say something to reassure her that all was safe. The footsteps stopped, and she could almost feel a set of sinister eyes probing the room. She felt shaky and could feel her heart beginning to pound, but desperate to remain hidden, she willed herself to breathe slowly and quietly while not moving a muscle.

After what seemed an eternity, the footsteps sounded again, this time retreating. She breathed a small sigh of relief and cautiously ventured a peek over the top of the grain barrel. What she saw did nothing to diminish her fear. The strange man was back in front of the store counter. He gestured wildly at the wagon in front of the store, and then slammed his fist on the counter. Vehemently he yelled, "I know there was a woman sitting on the seat of that wagon out front! I saw her! She must have come in here!"

The store owner's own voice was raised slightly as he replied meekly yet firmly, "No, no, she didn't, not since early this afternoon. They were both in here earlier, but then they left together. I believe they may have gone to the saloon! I ain't seen 'em since." He lowered and shook his head as his voice trailed off.

Fearful that the man would return to the storage room and look for her more closely, Jennifer eyed the back door that exited to the outside. Whatever she might find out there couldn't be worse than a man toting a gun while looking for her in here. In a state of mild panic, she stood upright and slowly edged toward the door. As she feared, she could still see the two men, but fortunately neither was looking in her direction. Quietly sliding the bolt to unlock the door, she stole one last glance at the men before pushing the door open slowly, praying it wouldn't squeak, and praying that the man would not turn and see her.

Moments later she found herself outside the store, wondering which way to run. *God, help me!* To her right was only an open field, but to her left a side road ran between the general store and the saloon. At the end of the store and saloon properties, the road took a left turn and ran behind the saloon and other town businesses. A few small houses were on the other side of the road. She focused on the houses. *Which one, Lord, which door shall I knock on? Is there anyone here who can help me?*

A small dog suddenly appeared and began to scratch and whine at the door of one of the small houses. *Lord, I am going to take that as a sign!* Jennifer ran quickly, crossing the road and joining the little dog at the doorway. The little dog turned and woofed slightly as he wagged his tail at her, but then he turned back to the door and continued to scratch and whine. Suddenly the door opened and Jennifer found herself staring down at a short, elderly woman who was looking for her pet.

"There you are, Sammy! Such a good little – oh my, who are you?" As her pet happily scampered inside, the startled woman stepped back in alarm at the sight of a strange young woman standing on the small porch. Before Jennifer could answer her, she added fearfully, "You don't have a gun, do you?"

"No, no, I don't have a gun, but there's a man after me and he has a gun, and I'm scared, and could I just come inside? I can't find my brother!" Jennifer tried to control the panic in her voice but she knew she wasn't succeeding.

The alarm on the woman's face turned to a scowl. "Oh dear, those west end boys, always up to no good! Well, you can come in just for a minute til I kin think what to do, 'cause I ain't gitten mixed up in anything to do with the likes of those scoundrels!" Her eyes flashed darkly as she grabbed Jennifer's hand and pulled her inside. After a quick look around at what could be seen of the town from the doorway, the woman quickly closed the door and locked it. "Sit yerself down over there!" She pointed to a cushioned chair, and Jennifer gladly dropped into it.

The sweet-faced elderly woman was attired in a long, full-skirted gray dress which buttoned up the front to a white lace collar, and was partly covered by a simple blue and white calico apron. Wire rimmed spectacles rested on her nose. Her silver gray hair was pulled back into a tight bun. Jennifer tried to keep quiet for a moment as the woman appeared to be mulling over the situation.

"You say you have a brother?"

Jennifer nodded. "Yes, my brother and I came to this town together in our wagon."

"And you can't find him? Why can't you find him?"

"Well, you see, we arrived in town early this afternoon, and we went into the general store and bought some supplies. Then Russell – that's my brother – he went into the saloon to see if he could find some work while I organized the supplies in our wagon. He said he'd be right back."

The woman smiled and looked relieved. "Oh, well, there's your answer, sweetie, he's just in the saloon kickin' back and havin' a beer with the fellas, that's all! Nothin' to worry yourself about!" Still smiling, she nodded as though she had just solved a mystery along with all of Jennifer's problems.

"No, he wouldn't do that." When the woman stopped smiling and stared at her skeptically, Jennifer continued, "He wouldn't leave the horses hitched up to the wagon and tethered in the sun all day. Besides, after he hadn't come back in a long time, I went over and looked into the saloon, and he's not in there, and then I went back into the general store and talked to the store owner, and a man with a gun started poking around our wagon, and the store owner told me to hide, so I did, and the man and the store owner started to argue, and then I slipped out the back door, and – well, here I am." Tears began to well up.

"Oh, I see, I see. Well now dearie, don't cry, surely there must be somethin' we can do." The woman stood still for a moment, obviously contemplating what she should do, and then she walked over to a coat and hat stand near the door. "Now then dearie, you jest sit tight," she said with a reassuring smile as she removed her apron and hung it on the stand. Then she removed a bonnet from the stand and pulled it onto her head. As she tied the ribbons of the bonnet under her chin she said, "I'm goin' to get help. You lock the door after me, and if anyone comes knockin' you'd best look out the winder afor you let 'im in!"

With that she was out the door, and Jennifer let the tears she had been trying to hold back run freely down her face.

CHAPTER FOUR

Jennifer sat until the tears stopped and she felt somewhat collected. She hoped the woman would return soon, although she didn't have any idea what anyone could do about the situation. *That little lady certainly wouldn't be a match for that man with the gun!* Jennifer shuddered at the thought.

Hearing the little dog nearby lapping water, she stood up with a despondent sigh and walked a few feet until she could see into the kitchen where the dog was drinking from a bowl on the floor. On seeing Jennifer, he left the water and scampered toward her, wagging his tail and woofing.

"Well, Sammy," Jennifer said as she reached down and patted his head, "You sure are a friendly little feller! Where do you suppose that mum of yours has gone off to? And I don't suppose you know where my brother is, do you?" Sammy's only response was more tail wagging and woofing.

As Jennifer settled back onto the chair, the little dog trotted to a folded blanket on the floor in a corner of the room and curled up to sleep. She watched him for a few moments, thinking it almost odd that he could curl up like that and contentedly fall asleep as though nothing were amiss. *Obviously, Sammy, you don't know that something is very wrong around here. I envy you in a way. I'd like to just curl up somewhere and fall asleep, and dream this whole nightmare completely away. None of this makes any sense and I just can't even begin to think where Russell might be!*

"Lord," she whispered aloud in prayer, "You know where Russell is. Please protect him, and please help us!" Restlessly she stood up again and went to the window. Pulling aside the curtain just a little, she could see the backs of the businesses that lined the main street of the town. She looked to the side road that ran between the store and the saloon, hoping to have at least a glimpse of the wagon and horses, but she couldn't see them at all. She could hear muffled sounds of laughter and music coming from the saloon. As she watched, the back door to the saloon suddenly swung open and a bartender heaved out a pail of sudsy water. For a moment she could hear the brassy piano music and laughter more loudly, then the bartender went back inside closing the door and the sounds were as muffled as before.

Turning away from the window and sitting down again, she tried to remain still and think, but none of what was happening made any sense so she focused instead on her surroundings. As she looked around the room she felt a little surprised at the modern furnishings. The room was decorated much like many of the modest yet comfortable homes she was accustomed to back east. It seemed a bit peculiar to find even a hint of luxury in this remote prairie land. She noted for the first time the wood floors and large throw rug in front of the fireplace. A sofa with ornate pillows and a lacey coverlet graced the wall across from her. A fireplace covered most of the wall separating the sitting room from the kitchen. A clock on the mantle revealed the lateness of the day, nearly 4 p.m. *Lord, is it really that late? Whatever has happened to Russell?*

A sudden noise from outside drew her attention and she quickly returned to the window. "I hear horses, Sammy!" She looked again at the side road and wished she could see the road in front of the store. She heard some shouting, and then there was the thudding sound of horse hooves and the clattering noise of a wagon being pulled away. Jennifer's heart dropped. "No, Lord, please, not our wagon! It has everything we own in it!"

Quickly she opened the door and stepped outside. Hoisting her long skirts a bit, she ran along the road behind the businesses until she came to a point where she could see the main road as it wound out of the small town and continued west. Just as she feared, their wagon was being driven away, accompanied by two strange men on horseback. She couldn't see clearly who was driving the wagon, but she was quite sure it was not Russell; he never would have whipped the horses to make them go so fast. She was sure the driver must be the same man with a gun who had been poking around their wagon and then had come into the general store looking for her.

Fearing the men might see her, she quickly retreated back into the house. Dazed, she sat back down on the chair briefly, but then got up and began to anxiously pace back and forth. "God, you have to help us!" She prayed out loud and fervently. "God, we need Your help! You have to do something!" Then words failed her; she simply could think of nothing else to pray aloud. *What would Mother do now? She would have said that it doesn't help much to fret and carry on when you find yourself in trouble. Rather, you need to calm down and just tell the Lord what you need, and ask for it in Jesus' name. He already knows exactly what you need anyway. And you should always remember God loves you and He can take care of everything! That's what Mother*

Calming herself a bit, Jennifer sat once again on the chair and began to pray aloud again, but with as much composure as she could muster. "Lord, I'm not sure exactly what else to pray. Russell and I need Your help, and although I don't even know what to ask You for, I know that You see the situation we are in, and I do sincerely ask You for the help You know we need, and I ask it in Jesus' name!" She sat still for a while, aching inside but realizing that there was absolutely nothing she could do, at least at this moment in time. However, deep inside she also felt a calming sense of somehow knowing that God had heard her cries.

Suddenly, the sound of voices drew her once again to the window. As she drew aside the curtains, she saw that the elderly woman was returning, and she seemed to be in quite a hurry. Jennifer felt a bit surprised that she could actually move that fast, given her age. She was being followed by several others, a younger woman and three men, one of whom Jennifer recognized as being the owner of the general store. She quickly unlocked the door, and then returned to the window to watch as they approached. The store owner and others didn't seem to be in quite the same haste as the older woman, but rather seemed to be trying to have a conversation as they walked. Then the younger woman called out, "Aunt Clara, do please slow down! Don't say anything!"

Clara ignored the request and sped up. Bursting through the door, she fixed her dark, sharp eyes on Jennifer and blurted out, "Your brother's dead! He's dead all right!"

Stunned, Jennifer stared silently as the room filled with people. They were all talking at once, but Jennifer could not make out a single word they said. She continued to stare in shock at Clara until the sound of all the voices faded, and the room began to spin before dimming and going completely black.

Jennifer had a vague realization that she had somehow gone from standing to lying down as she slowly returned to consciousness. She heard voices around her, but they were subdued, as if they were coming from far away. *Something terrible has happened, what was that? No, it was just a dream.* A memory was rising to the surface, but then it faded again. *Where am I? What is that awful smell? Smelling salts, oh no!* Opening her eyes was difficult, but she managed a brief glance before her eyelids closed heavily again. She made a feeble effort to push the smelling salts away as jumbled thoughts beset her. *Who are these people? Oh, yes, that little woman, now I know her name is Clara, and this is her house, and she has just said something terrible – what did she say? No, dear Lord, it can't be true, Russell can't really be dead.*

Her eyes flew open as she suddenly fully remembered Clara's stunning announcement. She realized she was lying on the sofa and found herself staring into the sympathetic eyes of the younger woman who had come into the house with the men. Grabbing the woman's arm, she blurted out, "My brother – he's not…"

The woman quickly reassured her, "No, no, dear, of course he's not." She patted Jennifer's arm consolingly as she sat next to her in a chair pulled up beside the sofa. "You fainted there, dear, but don't you worry, everything's going to be alright."

"Oh, he's dead alright, I saw him, blood on his shirt and all," Clara insisted as Jennifer turned her head enough to see the older woman standing by.

Eyes wide, Jennifer looked back to the younger woman in anguish.

The younger woman looked at Clara and said pointedly, "Aunt Clara, now would be a good time for you to make some tea for your guests, don't you think?"

"Well, if you think they'd like some, I'm more 'n happy to make it."

The younger woman watched Clara turn and go into the kitchen before looking back to Jennifer and speaking in a hushed tone, "I won't try to hide the truth from you, honey. Your brother got into a scrape with – well, shall we say, some of the less than friendly types around these parts – you know, the west end boys?" She scrutinized Jennifer as if to see if she understood at all. When Jennifer continued to stare incredulously and without any comprehension, she continued, "But the important thing for you to know is that he is alive, and he is with the doctor who is doing everything he can to make sure he stays that way. Doc has bandaged him up, and he believes he'll be just fine with a few days of rest and recuperation."

The tears Jennifer had been trying to hold back spilled over. Between sobs she cried out, "Russell never harmed a soul, why would anybody do anything to hurt him?"

The younger woman handed Jennifer a handkerchief and tried to console her. "Now, honey, don't you carry on so. It will be okay."

The store owner came out of the kitchen where he had been sitting and talking in hushed tones with the other men. "You lit out the back of my store just in time, little lady. I'm glad you found Clara's house. There's some others around here wouldn't be much help in a time like this. Too fearful to look out for anybody but themselves." Glancing back toward the kitchen, his voice almost became a whisper. "Now, Clara here, she's of the opinion that your brother is dead. She saw him lyin' unconscious on the doc's table, and we all have good reasons to let her go right on thinking that he has, in fact, passed on. Mainly, truth is, she can't keep a secret, no time, no how, and if them west end boys find out he ain't really dead, they may be inclined to come back and try to finish the job. I don't mean to scare you none, but you gotta deal with the facts as they are."

Jennifer looked from the store owner and then back to the younger woman. "I want to see my brother," she said after she wiped the tears off and blew her nose. "I need to see him."

The woman patted her arm again and said, "Of course you do dear, but first you need to gather a little strength back after fainting like that. A bit of tea will do you some good. And we will have to make sure it's safe and private when you do see him. It will take just a day or two of patience, dear."

The room grew silent as Clara returned bringing a teapot and some cups on a tray. After dutifully serving everyone a cup of the hot beverage, she set the tray on a nearby table. Jennifer sat up straight so she could sip from the cup without spilling.

Clara fixed her eyes on Jennifer. "Where's she gonna sleep? She has to sleep somewhere. How 'bout she stays here with me? She can sleep in the little back bedroom." The woman seemed quite hopeful.

The younger woman replied, "That's very kind of you, Aunt Clara, but I'm going to take her home with me. Her wagon is gone, and she'll be needing clothes. I think I have some things that will fit her. Sarah Lynn is stirring a pot of stew on the woodstove, and it won't be any trouble for me to feed the poor dear a bit of supper. Of course, you're welcome to come along as well, Clara dear. You're all welcome."

She paused for a moment, and when Clara returned to the kitchen with the empty tray, she quietly added, "By the way, dear, my name is Stella, and the storeowner here is Bart. The other gentlemen are Stephen and Charles. My husband Ben is with Doc and your brother right now."

The men nodded and smiled in welcome toward Jennifer. Still sniffling, she nodded back and replied, "I'm pleased to make your acquaintance." It was a mechanical statement, the truth being that she wasn't feeling pleased about anything whatsoever, except for her relief that Russell was not dead after all.

As Jennifer stared at the coffin being lowered into a freshly dug grave, she couldn't help but think it was a grim contrast to the peaceful surroundings. It was a beautiful day. A few fluffy white clouds dotted a clear blue sky. Birds sang from nearby trees. A gentle breeze helped to offset the heat of the noonday sun. Voices sang out a hymn in unison. "Though weeping may last through the night, shouts of joy will be heard at the break of day!"

When the singing was finished, Stella elbowed Jennifer gently and whispered, "If you don't start to at least cry a bit, I'm going to have to pinch you!"

Jennifer stifled a giggle. "It's hard to feel grieved over a coffin full of rocks!" she whispered back.

"I know it is, but just the same you need to act the part. Sharp eyes are watching!"

Jennifer let out a feigned sob and dabbed her eyes with a handkerchief as she glanced first at those gathered for the funeral, and then at the strange man on horseback watching vigilantly from a nearby hillside. "Is he one of the west end boys?" she whispered anxiously.

"Yes, dear, but don't you worry none. He's not here to hurt anyone; he's just spying out the facts for the rest of them. Just cry a bit, now, Aunt Clara's watching you like a hawk!" Jennifer feigned another sob as Stella's arm reached around her consolingly. "There, there now, you poor dear!"

A brief glance in Clara's direction confirmed Stella's words; the older woman's keen eyes were narrowed and fixed relentlessly on Jennifer from across the open grave. Jennifer tried to cry as if she were inconsolable, but she found it difficult to manage as she thought about her brother who even now was probably sitting up in bed enjoying a cup of coffee. *I will have fun relating the events of his funeral to him later. Don't think about that! Right now I need to cry! Why is it that tears never come easily when they aren't real?*

The pastor from the town's only church began to say a few words to honor the deceased and comfort the bereaved. He seemed like a nice pastor and Jennifer felt sure her mother would have approved of him. His wife and two small children stood nearby, surrounded by a few of the town folk, including the two women Jennifer had watched from the wagon as they walked into the general store – *had it really been only a few short days ago?* Today they didn't wear the disapproving expressions as before, but looked sympathetic. She wondered if their sympathies were sincere, or if perhaps they were in on the conspiracy to make her brother appear to be deceased. *How many of these people here know?* She glanced furtively at everyone from under slightly teary lashes.

Thoughts of the deception she was involved in caused

her to wonder if all lies were sin. She had been raised to believe they surely were, and yet she also felt her dear mother would have approved, if only in this very instance. Stella's husband Ben had reassured her it was the only way to keep Russell safe, and therefore it was the only right thing to do. She knew he was right, but nevertheless she prayed about it silently. *Lord, I do feel a bit guilty about hiding the truth from all these good folk, but You know we just don't have a choice. Still, I ask Your forgiveness.* The most important thing her mother had always tried to teach her was that being a Christian was much more about walking in a real relationship with the living God than it was about religious rules and such.

She tried to focus on the words of the pastor. "Now we all here didn't know the departed man, Russell, but I am assured by his dear sister that he was our brother in the Lord, and we shall all have the privilege to meet him in the by and by when we shall go to be with our Lord." He paused and cleared his throat. "The Bible tells us plainly that we are made right with God by the atoning blood of His Son, Jesus, on the cross, and it is by His sacrifice and suffering that we are cleansed from all sin. And it is because of His own resurrection that we ourselves are guaranteed of our own resurrection to life eternal, to live forevermore with Him in heaven." He paused and looked around at the group as if waiting to let his words sink in. "If there should happen to be any soul here who is not sure of their own salvation, I invite you to stay and visit with me after the service. I would like to share with you how you can know that God loves you, and your sins are forgiven, and how you can know that God has a place reserved for you in heaven."

After another pause, the pastor opened his Bible and began to read, "*These things have I written unto you that believe on the name of the Son of God; that ye may know that ye have eternal life, and that ye may believe on the name of the Son of God.*' This reading is 1 John 5:13 from the King James. Now let us say the Lord's Prayer together, "*Our Father, which art in heaven…*"

Even as she somewhat mechanically mouthed the words to the prayer, Jennifer's thoughts wandered again, and this time she was praying silently, thanking God that Russell was not really dead. Although her prayer was genuine, the thankful feelings quickly gave way to a sense of foreboding that nudged its way to the surface of her thoughts once again. It was the same nagging fear she now shared with her new friends, the people of Wolcott. Their enemy was now her enemy, and the dread she felt was like a shadowy, evil presence that could not be reasoned away. Her eyes shifted from the coffin to the hillside, and she watched as the rider finally reined his horse aside and rode away over the hill.

CHAPTER FIVE

Jennifer smiled as she sat on the edge of the porch and watched the younger three of Stella's six children playing in the yard. The youngest was only fourteen months old, yet he determinedly toddled about, ignoring Jennifer's gentle warnings to stay close. "No, Stevie, that mother hen will peck you!" she said when he tottered too close to a hen who was busily scratching in the dirt. Stevie's plump little hands reached out to grab a chick, and although he failed to grasp his prize, just as Jennifer had warned, the hen practically flew to ward off the apparent threat to her chick. Undeterred, he reached out to grab the hen herself, and received a mild peck on his hand. "No, no, bad hen," Jennifer scolded as she scooped the whimpering toddler up and kissed away his hurt. Clucking fussily, the hen gathered her brood under her wings and hustled them away.

Jennifer brought Stevie closer to the house and sat him down to play in the dirt along with Jason and Marie. Jason was making little roads for a toy wooden wagon while Marie propped up a rag doll in the dirt and warned her not to soil her pretty new dress. Jason was five years old and Marie three. Jennifer couldn't help but marvel at their sweet innocence and obliviousness to life in general around them. They understood nothing of the so-called 'west end boys' and the danger lurking in the town where they lived. They cared about toys and their Mommy and simple things like a drink of 'wahwah' as Marie called it, or the occasional sweet treat from the general store. As for Jennifer, they accepted the newcomer with shy enthusiasm, happy to have someone new to show a favorite doll or toy wagon to.

Stella's older girls, Sara Lynn, fourteen, and Dorinda, thirteen, were helping their mother pick beans in the garden while the oldest, a boy of seventeen named Seth, was helping out by working on the fencing for the ranch's cattle herd. For the most part, Seth ignored Jennifer. He exhibited the awkward shyness of a young man not accustomed to being around an attractive young woman, and never said more than a few words to her at a time. The girls, however, were excited to have a new friend, even though she was a few years older, and drew her in to their chatter and giggling whenever possible.

Soon the bean picking was finished, and Stella brought washed beans in a strainer for Jennifer to help string and stem. At their mother's request, the girls went into the house to prepare lunch. Settling on the porch beside Jennifer, Stella said, "I know I promised to explain the situation here in Wolcott. I said I'd tell you the whole story, and this seems as good a time as any. Stevie, don't put that in your mouth, no, no!"

"No, no!" Stevie echoed his mother and dropped something back into the dirt.

"Here's a paring knife, dear. Now if you cut off the top at a slant, the string comes off – yes, just like that. You know, Wolcott wasn't always such a bad town. It started off quite well. Truth is, it's partly named after Richard Wolcott, and he just happens to be the leader of that pack of snakes we've come to call the west end boys."

"But wasn't Wolcott your father's name too?" Jennifer asked hesitantly.

Stella sighed. "Yes, it most surely was. The fact is that Richard Wolcott is my uncle, and there's not a day goes by I don't agonize over that. You see, dear, my father, God rest his soul, was Samuel Wolcott, the younger of the two brothers. After my grandparents died, they came out west together with the inheritance Grandfather had left the two of them. They staked out big land claims and built big houses – this right here being my father's and the one out west of town being Richard's. They had lots of money, so they both hired hands to raise cattle for them. They both married and went to raisin' young 'uns. Life on the prairie is never easy, but they had enough money to make it easier. The town needed a livery stable, so the two of them paid to haul in lumber and have it built. We needed a general store, so it was built. The whole town more or less grew up around them. People would own the businesses by arranging to pay my uncle and father back over time. It seemed life all around was pretty good. There was a time when we even had grand parties, mostly at my uncle's house. He was quite the social gadabout back in that day. He liked to show off his wife, Lucille. She was quite the pretty thing, and very outgoing herself."

"So, what happened to change all that?"

"Mainly, things started to go badly when Aunt Lucille got real sick. Uncle Richard already drank more 'n he ought to have before that, but when she didn't get well and then she up and died, well, he just completely fell apart. I don't think he wanted to live without her, so he hid himself behind the whiskey bottle. My five cousins, all boys, grew up pretty wild after that. He didn't really seem to care what they did, so they just did pretty much whatever they pleased. Oh, he'd lose his temper with them a lot, especially when he was drinkin' extra hard, but he didn't really do anything consistently to discipline them, you know? They just didn't get the strict moral upbringin' they needed, nor the basic love and attention that any good parent gives his child."

Jennifer nodded. "But still, how could they get this whole town terrorized the way it is?"

Stella sighed. "Those boys used to come into town and drink and gamble in the saloon all the time. They got into a little trouble here and there. My father used to try to have talks with his brother about their behavior. Tried to get him to put the bottle away, even tried to get him and the boys into church, but mostly it didn't seem to do much good." Stella paused and shrugged. "Don't really know what he or anybody else around here could have done. Anyway, one of Richard's boys took a liken' to a pretty girl in town. So, I guess you could say that what really started it all was a crime of passion. He stole an expensive painting right off the wall of his father's house, and brought it to her as a gift. Seems she didn't care quite as much for him as he did for her, though, because she joked about his gift to friends of theirs, particularly another boy. One night that boy and my cousin got into it over the girl and that silly painting, can you imagine that? And my cousin was so mad he up and shot that other fella! The boy was only eighteen years old and he died right there on the spot!" Stella took a hankie out and dabbed her eyes.

"I'm sorry, Stella. I didn't mean to make you cry telling me the story."

"Oh, sweetie, it gets much worse, I'm sure this hankie will be soaked by the time I get done tellin' it all to you!"

The conversation was interrupted suddenly as the women saw Clara approaching with her little dog, Sammy. "What are you two talkin' about?" was her blunt greeting as she arrived somewhat out of breath at the front porch. "Sammy, sit! Don't you chase them chickens!" After scolding Sammy, she turned her sharp gaze back on Jennifer and Stella. Sammy sat down obediently and woofed now and then as he stared at the hen and her brood of chicks.

Stella replied, "Nothing in particular, Clara, dear. Just chatting about things while we string the beans." She stood up and gave Clara a quick hug. "How nice of you to visit. The girls are fixing lunch, won't you join us?"

"Well, 'course I will." Clara turned her keen eyes again toward Jennifer. "She sad on account o' her brother bein' dead? She don't cry all that much!"

"What a thing to ask! Of course she's sad, Clara!"

"Well, I don't mean to be disrespectful. Jest seems ever time I look at 'er she's not carryin' on all that much."

"She's just being very brave. And my, what a help she's been to me with the children and all. Now why don't we all go inside and see if that lunch is ready! Come on children, lunch time! Who wants to ring the bell for Seth?"

Jason and Marie both began to fuss, "I do, Mommy, I do!"

"Now, now, settle down, you can each have a turn." She picked Jason up and held him while he pulled determinedly on the rope to the dinner bell and squealed in delight when the bell rang out. Putting him back on the porch, she picked up Marie and gave her a turn, after which they both ran laughing into the house.

Turning away from Clara's scrutiny, Jennifer picked up Stevie and carried him into the house. She snuggled him tightly as her thoughts turned to the situation she and her brother found themselves caught up in. *I really ought to be crying anyway! My brother's hurt and our wagon and horses have been stolen. Lord, I don't know just how troubled Russ is feeling about all this, but as for me, I sometimes feel so disheartened I nearly cannot take another breath. If not for the kindness of these dear folk, I don't know what we would have done. Lord, this all hurts, but still I'm so thankful for Stella and this family, and for all You are doing to get us through this.* She realized that somehow in spite of all her anxious thoughts and fears she still had an underlying sense of trust and even hope.

As Jennifer placed Stevie into his wooden high chair and tied a long piece of cloth around him to keep him from squirming out, she looked around at the spacious open room. It was very unlike the lacy interior of Clara's small house. Rather, it was somewhat rugged and practical, yet invitingly comfortable and homey. She thought about how soundly she had slept the previous night in the large feather bed, and how ungrudgingly Dorinda had given up her own room, sharing a room with Sara Lynn so that Jennifer could have a place to sleep. They were all so friendly toward her that it was difficult to feel sad about anything for very long. Her sense of fear only came fully into focus when she thought about the west end boys. How surprised she was to learn that Stella was actually related to them! She washed Stevie's little hands with a soapy cloth, and shortly they were all seated, bowing their heads in thanks for the meal.

When lunch was over, Dorinda and Sara Lynn cleaned up the kitchen while Seth went back to resume work on the fence and the women set about to get the little ones to take their naps. Shortly all the little ones were asleep and even Clara was lying on the sofa snoring softly. Dorinda and Sara Lynn retreated to their room to read for a while and Stella and Jennifer quietly slipped out the front door to continue their conversation on the porch.

With a sigh, Stella began, "Did I tell you my father was the sheriff in town at that time?"

"No, I don't think you mentioned it."

"Wolcott being a small town, we didn't often have too much trouble, but someone needed to take up the office, and my father was willing to take it on. Well, when my cousin realized what he had done, he lit out for home. Most of the town folk along with Judge Carter gathered together, and after the body of the deceased young man had been given over to his folks and the doc, they all agreed my father had to go after his own nephew and arrest him for the murder. There were witnesses to the shooting, so there wasn't really any question exactly who had done it. Seemed everyone had simply had enough of the grief caused by those boys, and they just weren't about to put up with any more of it!"

Stella sighed again before continuing, "Several of the men from town, including my first husband, went with Father, as deputies in an unofficial sense, but by the time they got out there, my Uncle Richard, him bein' pretty drunk as usual, was waitin' on the front porch with my cousins all crowded in behind him. My father and the others dismounted from their horses, and went up to the porch to talk to him. My father said they'd come to arrest the boy, and he'd just best hand him over. Uncle Richard did some yellin' about nobody goin' to take his son away from him. Well, no one really knows for sure who fired the first shot – the report later was that it seemed mostly just random shots fired into the air to scare off the deputies, but when it was all done, my father and my first husband were both lying dead on the ground." Stella's hankie came back out and she wiped away the tears that were streaming down her cheeks.

"You lost both your father and your husband on the same day?" Jennifer asked with deep sympathy as she wiped the tears from her own eyes.

"Yes, I surely did." Stella blew her nose and waited a bit before saying, "Don't really know what happened to that cousin of mine. Some say he lit out for Mexico. Could be he ended up back at the ranch, some say they have seen him. Anyway, most of the rest of the boys just went from bad to worse. They started up riding into town often, shooting at anybody that tried to resist them and stealing whatever they needed to live on."

"Why don't they just come in to town and shoot everybody?"

"The irony is that they need this town. They let their own ranch go to the devil, purely too lazy to run it right. So they just come in here and take whatever they want at gunpoint. And the truth is that it's not even just my uncle and cousins that live out there any more. Every once in a while some new worthless feller with nothin' better to do with himself joins up with them. They've even brought in a couple of well, shall we say ladies of a lesser reputation? And now some of those fellers have young children. I feel so badly for the little ones; can you imagine bein' born and brought up in that den of thieves?"

Jennifer shook her head and sighed. "Don't any of the town's people have guns so they can make them stop?"

"Guns were one of the first things they started in stealin'. Oh, there's a few left, but generally whenever those boys come into town they stick together, and nobody's brave nor foolish enough to take on the lot of 'em."

"Then what's to be done?"

"Not sure I can answer that. We've tried things – like sending some of our own boys to Newton, a bigger town up north of here, to ask for help. They sent in a sheriff and a couple of deputies. The west end boys shot at them, wounding the sheriff and one of the deputies. Chased them back where they came from. Seems no one wants to help us now. Can't really blame them. Oh, we still make plans to take the town back, but sometimes I think making plans is just another way to avoid actually doing something. Fact is, Ben and the store owner Bart, Judge Carter, Doc and a few others right now are having another meeting, making more plans. Don't mention it to Clara, now, of course."

Jennifer smiled. "She's quite the spirited one, isn't she?"

Stella laughed, "Yes, she surely is!"

"But she's your aunt, is she a Wolcott, too?"

"Oh no, she's from my mother's side. You see, my mother and Clara came out west with my grandparents when they were still young girls. Eventually my mother met and married my father, but Clara never married, and so after my grandparents and parents had all passed on, she lived with us for quite some time. Then we had that little house built so she could have her own place with some peace and quiet, but Clara is still over here as much as she is in her own home, I think. I don't mind. She's helpful with the children, and when she's here I don't have to worry about her being alone so much, especially now that she's getting on in years."

Jennifer was thoughtful for a few minutes. "I don't think I could manage all this like you have. You work so hard here on your ranch, and you're so brave in the face of the danger here. I think I would have found a way to move away from here a long time ago!"

"Many have done just that, they've given up and moved back east or even further west. Can't say I never thought about it. But I will tell you straight out, I believe this is the home God has for me. If I didn't believe He was right here with me, I don't think I would have had the courage to stay and marry Ben and have more children. In that regard I don't regret at all the way things have turned out, because I can't even begin to tell you how much I love Ben and our children!"

She paused thoughtfully before saying, "You know Jennifer, life is never easy. Even if the town hadn't been troubled by the west end boys, prairie life can be tough. Winters are cold, summers are hot and at times too dry to grow any decent crops. We've lost livestock in blizzards, and watched good seed sprout only to dry up and die in the fields. The one thing I know is that God has been with us through it all, He has surely provided for all of our needs!

CHAPTER SIX

Jennifer glanced around a bit nervously as she made her way to the doctor's house. She was carrying a basket of freshly baked bread and some beef stew Stella had made. She didn't mind if people thought she and Stella were just being neighborly toward the doc and all, but it would surely do no good if certain ones of the town folk realized she was actually bringing food to her brother who was supposedly deceased. A few children and a dog were playing in the street, but no one else was about, so she tried to focus on enjoying the sunshine and singing birds as she walked. *It really is a beautiful day, Lord. I am thankful for the sunshine. Most of all I am so very, very thankful for the fact that Russell is healing up, and I do pray that You would continue to make him completely well.*

She arrived at the small house which was also the town's only doctor's office in a matter of minutes and was greeted warmly by Greta, the doctor's wife. "Russell will be glad to see you dear, it's been a couple of days!" Although she said that, they both understood Jennifer didn't dare visit more often as it could raise suspicions. Greta led the way down a darkened hallway and tapped lightly on a door. A muffled, "Come in," was the response from inside the room.

"Good morning," Greta greeted Russell cheerily as she opened the door. "You have a visitor!" She stepped aside and allowed Jennifer into the room, then closed the door behind her.

Jennifer was pleasantly surprised to see her brother up, fully dressed and sitting on a chair. "You're up!" she exclaimed.

Putting aside the Bible he had been reading, Russell stood up, wincing slightly and holding his rib cage. Then he kissed her lightly on the forehead and said, "Jen, it's so good to see you! Don't get many visitors here. Mm, that smells good!" He smiled as she placed the basket of food on the small table next to the chair he had been sitting in.

"You must be feeling a whole lot better. Couple days ago you were still in bed!"

"Doc says it's better if I get up and move around a bit now." He moved his arms about in a stretching motion, but stopped and winced again at the pain in his ribs. "Still hurts pretty much, but he says I'm mendin' up just fine."

"Oh, Russ, I am so relieved and thankful! You know, I've learned a lot about the boys who roughed you up. From what I've been told, they surely are a wicked gang of ruffians! Apparently the act we put on for your funeral worked, though, because I've heard that they sure enough think you're dead!"

"Yeah, that's what I'm told." Russell adjusted the bandage that wrapped around his head. "Surely a dismal state of affairs, the way they've got this whole town bullied and scared."

Jennifer thought back for a moment before she asked,

"You already knew about the west end boys, didn't you? You know, before we came into town. It's what was bothering you, wasn't it? I could tell something was on your mind that you didn't want to talk about."

"Yeah, I gotta admit that was bothering me, quite a lot, actually. Jerome told me about them, and he even went so far as to say we might oughta just leave our wagon and everything in it behind and let some of the good folks make some room for us in their wagons. But there wouldn't have been room for our stuff, and it just didn't seem like a good idea to leave every single thing we owned behind."

"You never told me. I thought he didn't try to offer us any help just because I wouldn't marry him!"

"Well, there was that. After we'd talked about things for a while, he did up and say something to the effect that after all that time you still hadn't agreed to marry him anyway. Almost like he was giving up on that notion and just taking the easiest way out as far as keeping us together with the wagon train. But he also said he couldn't wait around and deal with our problem because he had a responsibility to get the rest of the folks dropped off up north. I actually couldn't disagree with that. So, yes, he did warn me about that gang of outlaws. Then when the Indian showed up with the horse, he mentioned the outlaws too, just wanting to warn us about how things were around these parts. I didn't mention it to you because I didn't see any good reason for you to be worrying about it too."

"Russell, you always try to carry all the heavy responsibility yourself. I don't know what I could have done, probably nothing, but still, maybe somehow it would have helped if we had talked about it."

"Maybe. But I just didn't want you to be any more

worried than you already were." He sighed before adding a bit glumly, "The way it's turned out I guess it didn't do us any good to try to hold onto the stuff and the wagon after all, now that it's all been stolen." He sighed and shook his head dejectedly, but then he abruptly lifted his chin. Looking at Jennifer with an affectionate smile, he said, "Well, enough of that gloomy business. How are you doin,' Jen? Those folks still treating you good?"

"Oh, Russ, they have been so kind. But did you know Stella is cousin and niece to them west end boys?"

"Those west end boys, dear."

"You sound like Mom."

"Yep, someone's gotta teach you good English. And yes, I did know. Bart, the store owner, and some of the other fellers told me the whole story."

"Stella's been so kind to me. I hate to think of all the trouble and sadness she's had on account o' them. You know, she's had a hard life, mostly all because of them! But still, she's so kind and considerate of others." While she talked, Jennifer began to pull the bread and stew out of the basket and fix a plate for Russell.

"Yep, the town folk here have sure been good to us." Taking his seat at the table, he asked, "You gonna help me eat this? There's a lot here!"

"No, I already had some with Stella and the children. You know, it's too bad there isn't something that could be done to help the town out of this mess."

"Yeah, not to mention us!"

"Well, of course, we sure are in a mess. But I guess I just figured we'd head back east now, as soon as you are well enough to travel, I mean. Stella says there's a stagecoach coming through here fairly regular now."

Russell didn't answer, but began to stuff bread and stew into his mouth. "Mmm, this is great, little sis! You make it?"

"No, I can't take credit. Stella made it this morning while I watched the little ones. Did you know her children are from two different marriages? The older three are from her first marriage. Her husband was killed that awful day along with her father. Can you imagine losing your father and your husband on the same day, and by your own relative's hand at that?"

Russell sighed. "No, that's gotta be tough. But she has a good husband now, Ben, you know, he's a good Christian man, and the way he talks he sure loves them all."

"Yes, he's a good man! Oh, Russ, they have all simply stolen my heart, especially that little one, Stevie. He's a real sweetie! So full of energy and always into something, though. I think Stella appreciates a break from chasing after the little ones all the time. With me there, she can tend to the cooking and cleaning while I watch out for them."

"That's great, Sis, I'm proud of you for helping her out. I wish I could do something. Bit tired of hidin' out back here. I can't go near the windows, and I always gotta keep the light down low. I'm about ready to die of absolute boredom! At least I'm gettin' some reading done, though, that's a good thing."

"I know it's been rough for you, it surely has, but I'm so thankful you're feeling better." After a reflective pause Jennifer added, "Russ, you know you didn't answer me."

"Hmm?"

"About the stagecoach. About going home."

Russell avoided meeting her eyes as he replied unconcernedly, "Well, we'll have to see."

Jennifer's heart dropped. "Russell, you look at me! You cannot possibly be thinking there is any way we can stay on here, not after all that's happened!" She glared at him fiercely with her hands on her hips.

Amused at her indignation, he smiled and raised a finger to his lips. "Shh, gotta keep our voices down. Thin walls, you know!"

A few days later, Jennifer sat with Stella on a bench on the boardwalk in front of The Stagecoach Stop Hotel. They tried to make small talk as they watched people coming and going along the boardwalk. Complete with a small restaurant, the hotel was the largest business in Wolcott and usually bustling with activity.

"Well, if you must go, I do hope you will write," Stella said.

"Yes, I will. And will you let me know how things are – you know, with Russ and all?"

"Of course I will, dear."

"Hello, you two!" Stella and Jennifer turned toward the voice and watched as a woman hoisted her skirts a bit and made her way across the dusty street toward them. Her ample size made the short walk a bit of an effort, and she sounded somewhat out of breath as she asked, "How are you ladies doing this fine morning?"

Stella and Jennifer both replied at the same time, "Morning, Kathleen." Stella added, "We are well, and how are you this morning?"

Kathleen drew in a deep breath and patted her chest before answering, "Well, now, I'm doing just fine." She smiled amiably at both, then looked more soberly at Stella and pointedly asked, "Stella, have you talked to her yet?"

"Now, Kathleen, we have to let her make up her own mind. She has a mind to go back east, and you know we can't blame her."

Kathleen sighed heavily. "Yes, I know, but you said you'd talk to her again."

Jennifer had had the privilege of getting to know Kathleen mostly through the town's small church, and she loved her friendly disposition, bright outlook and quick wit. She laughed often and whole-heartedly, making people around her want to laugh along with her. At the moment, however, her demeanor seemed less than jovial, and Jennifer thought she even appeared a bit agitated.

As she listened to the two discussing her almost as if she were not present, Jennifer thought again about all the reasons she had for leaving. Nothing had gone right for her and Russell ever since they'd been left alone on the prairie a few weeks earlier. Even after they'd been supplied with a new horse to replace the one that had to be shot, they had only ended up getting in even worse trouble once they'd arrived in Wolcott. Not only had the west end boys stolen their horses and wagon, but they had beaten Russell nearly to death. Yet in spite of all that, now that Russell was healing up and getting his strength back, he simply refused to listen to reason and get on the stage to go back east. *How completely mule-headed can he be? Can't he see that we have ended up in the wrong place, and it is time to forget our dreams of a future out west and head back home?*

Jennifer shook her head in frustration as she remembered their last conversation. "I understand how you feel, and I won't stop you if you want to go back," Russell had said. "It may even be the best thing for you. You can get back together with our friends from the church back east, and I know they'll take good care of you. But I can't go. We've come this far, and I'm not backing down. I'm gonna stay right here and see if maybe I can help do something about the situation in this town."

"Stella, now don't you think for one little minute that I don't understand Jennifer's pain!" Kathleen's voice was rising fervently, drawing Jennifer's attention back to the present. "I know the danger here just as well as you! I can understand her need to go back home! But you know as well as I there is someone else in this town who's need is even greater than Jennifer's, and I just happen to think she might be grown up enough to understand that, and be willing to do the charitable thing here!"

It dawned on Jennifer that Stella had, in fact, tried to start a conversation earlier that morning. She had assumed all along it had only been another effort to talk her out of leaving. Now, as she listened to Kathleen she felt there must be something more to it than just that. "What are you talking about?" she asked Kathleen directly.

With a sigh, Kathleen placed a restraining hand on Stella's arm as she gave her a knowing look. Then she turned to face Jennifer and explained, "Child, I know you're hurting. You've come out here with high hopes, but nothin' has turned out like you dreamed it would. We all know the danger in this town, and that now you want to go home. Surely not a one of us would blame you for feeling that way. We even feel somewhat responsible, and that's why we all agreed to scrape up enough money to pay for the fare on the stagecoach."

She paused for a moment and looked around before she continued, "But the fact is, there's another here in Wolcott whose need is even greater than your own. She is a woman in a truly dire state of affairs, and she's on her way here right now. We've told her we'd all just be seein' you off, sayin' goodbye and all that. But the truth is, she needs to get outa here a whole lot worse than you do, and we can't afford to scrape up enough for another ticket at this time, and even if we could there isn't likely room for yet one more body on that coach. Child, do you understand what I am asking you?"

Stunned, Jennifer stared at Kathleen speechlessly. *Stay here in this dreadful town? Give the ticket to someone else?* Before she could collect her thoughts enough to reply, their conversation was interrupted by the arrival of Stella's children and Aunt Clara.

CHAPTER SEVEN

There was quite a commotion as Stella's children and Clara arrived on the boardwalk in front of the Stagecoach Stop Hotel. Sara Lynn carried Stevie, Dorinda carried little Marie and Clara led Jason by the hand. "Jenny, are you staying?" Sara Lynn asked hopefully and a bit out of breath as they all crowded around Jennifer.

"Are you staying, Jenny, did you change your mind? Please say you're going to stay!" Dorinda chimed in earnestly.

"Nenny, Nenny!" Stevie leaned determinedly toward Jennifer, almost forcing her to take him or watch him fall. Taking him with a sad smile, she hugged him tightly until he giggled. *Lord, I am going to miss these children – and this family, and all the friends we have here.*

Dorinda put Marie down, and she and Jason began to run back and forth on the boardwalk laughing in delight at the echoing sound made by their feet hitting the boards.

"She leavin' on account o' them west end boys?" Clara's

question was characteristically blunt, loud and addressed to no one in particular. Jennifer had come to realize that she was a bit hard of hearing, and probably without knowing it she spoke loudly as if all were as deaf as she.

All eyes were on Jennifer, waiting for answers, but she was nearly at a loss for words. "Yes, I'm going back east," was all she could manage.

Suddenly Jason started to cry, and Stella picked him up. "What's the matter, young man?" she asked as she brushed the tears from his face.

A tug on Jennifer's skirt made her look down at Marie, who was looking up solemnly at her. "My fault," she said quietly.

Glad for the distraction, Jennifer handed Stevie back to Sara Lynn and stooped down to gaze into three-year-old Marie's sad face. "What is your fault, sweetie?"

"I make Jathon cry," the toddler said quietly as she held out a small stick. "I poke him with thith. It wath akdent."

"It was an accident?"

The toddler nodded sadly. "Akdent." Then she shook her head and said, "I dint mean to."

Trying not to smile, Jennifer gently replied, "Okay sweetie, just tell him you're sorry."

Stella, having dried and kissed away Jason's tears, put him down in front of Marie. "I thorry." Marie made her quick apology and the two ran off to play together again.

The sound of trotting horse hooves and a clattering

buggy announced the arrival of Seth, Stella's oldest. He had a passenger with him, and the mysterious words Kathleen had spoken just minutes earlier suddenly became quite clear. Jennifer recognized the woman on the seat of the buggy as being Hannah, a very quiet and withdrawn woman she had become acquainted with through the town church. Stella and Kathleen had mentioned the woman's troubles before, but only briefly as neither was inclined toward gossip. Hannah's husband, in Stella's words, was the nicest man you'd ever want to meet, that is until he began to drink. Faint bruises on Hannah's thin face were evidence enough of the man's drunken rages.

The compassion Jennifer had felt for her rose again to the surface. That combined with her own present turmoil caused her eyes to sting with tears. As she thought about it, she realized she had been prone to tears the last few days like never in her life before. She had spent much of the previous night crying into her pillow and tossing restlessly as she brooded over her decision to leave Russell behind and get on the stagecoach. Even now she was uncertain she was making the right decision, and yet here she was, waiting for the coach. She blinked and held the tears back determinedly; crying now would not help and might upset the children.

Seth helped Hannah down from the buggy and tied the horse to the hitching rail as Hannah somewhat timidly approached the group on the boardwalk. Unsmiling, she said, "Good morning, everyone. Jennifer, it has been a pleasure to know you, and I do hope your journey is a safe and pleasant one." Her words were abrupt, delivered quickly as though rehearsed, and then she remained silent.

"Thank you," Jennifer replied quietly. "It's been a pleasure to know you as well."

Kathleen took a determined step toward Jennifer and said

pointedly, "You know, dear, Hannah has a sister and other relatives in Boston. She hasn't seen them for quite a long time, isn't that right, Hannah?"

"Yes," Hannah replied with a wistful look in her eyes. "I haven't seen my family since we came out here." She paused and stared off into the distance as though trying to remember just how long ago that had been. "Well, it's been several years, I don't remember just how long." Her voice trailed off, and after a moment of silence, she moved away from the group to take a seat on the nearby bench.

Kathleen turned her eyes back on Jennifer and doggedly repeated the question she had asked her only minutes earlier. "Child, do you understand what I am asking you to do?"

Jennifer could only nod silently.

Kathleen persisted, yet quietly so as not to be overheard by Hannah. "Now we all had a little chat with her husband in a sober moment, and he agreed that it would be in her best interests for her to go back home at least for a while. Stella and I gathered together a bag of clothing and things for her, and Seth has it stowed in the back of the buggy. If you will agree to let her go instead, she has everything she needs. Goodness child, think of the blessing it would be to her!"

Jennifer remembered the words of her mother, who had often told her that if she needed a moment to think before answering a question she should take it, because you can't always take back a careless or hasty response. Taking a deep breath she looked around at all present and said, "I need a minute to think."

Stella was quick to respond. "Of course you do, dear. Take all the time you need. Children, all of you, come here!

Let Jenny have a minute alone to think."

The children obediently gathered around their mother and watched as Jennifer gratefully moved away from them, stepping down from the boardwalk and walking a short distance away. *Sometimes it's best to take a few minutes alone to pray when you don't know what to do, Jennifer.* Her mother's words rang in her mind while turbulent emotions ran through her heart. She considered how much she missed her mother now, but even as she did, she also realized that Stella was so like her, and was surely the closest she had now to a mother's presence in her life. She might miss Stella most of all.

All, that is, except her brother, of course. Her angry feelings toward him had begun to dissipate, and she even felt she might be able to swallow her pride and relent on saying she would go back east without him if it came to that. *Lord, I can forgive and forget all that if you help me. And Lord, Hannah surely needs to get out of here. She'd be going back to family, and I'd actually be leaving family behind here. And the truth is my heart is breaking about that. What shall I do? Lord, I know you can give me an answer.*

More memories of her mother rose to the surface. *Jennifer, you should help people when you can, and remember that opportunities to do truly good deeds don't come along every day. Take advantage of them. You will not only help another, but you'll have peace because God is pleased when we prefer others over ourselves.* She sighed in frustration as she kicked a pebble aside. *But Lord, what about those west end boys? What about the danger lurking in this dusty, desolate town? What will happen if I stay?*

The sudden sound of more feet echoing on the boardwalk drew her attention. She gasped as she saw the man who had just come out of the hotel. It was none other than Jerome, the wagon master who had abandoned her and

Russell a few weeks earlier. She stared disbelievingly as he and two other men stepped away from the hotel doorway and remained standing about on the boardwalk. She recognized the other men as being Jerome's hired guards for the wagon train, and she wondered what they were doing here in the small town of Wolcott rather than out on the trail leading the wagons. She didn't relish encountering Jerome, and thought back to the day he had left them out on the trail. *I'll marry you!* That's all she would have had to say for him to work out the situation rather than to lead the wagon train onward without them.

Lord, help me! You know Jerome and I have been friends since childhood, but now I don't know what to say to this man! She thought then about what her mother might be inclined to say to her. *Holding a grudge will never be the right answer, Jen. You can always overcome bitterness with prayer and a forgiving heart.* With a determined sigh, she hoisted her skirts and headed back to the boardwalk. "Hello, Jerome." He turned in surprise at the sound of her voice.

"Jennifer! My dear, Jennifer, whatever are you still doin' way out here? I woulda thought you'd be back east by now." His voice trailed off as he saw the look of surprise registering on her face. Self-consciously, he gingerly touched his bruised and battered face.

Jennifer continued to look at him in alarm as she saw that his right arm was in a sling and a head bandage was not fully concealed by his hat. "Jerome, what on earth happened to you?" She tried to sound not overly concerned, mindful even now that his affection and intentions toward her might not have diminished, and she certainly had no intention of encouraging his unrequited feelings.

He hesitated, and in that moment Stella with her children, Clara and Kathleen all surrounded Jennifer once again, all talking at once. As usual, Clara's voice rang somewhat shrilly over the rest. "Dearie, do you know this man? Is he one o' them west-end boys? What happened to 'im? Does he have a gun?"

Deciding that this acquaintance could use an explanation, Jennifer spoke to all, "This is Jerome Smith, the wagon master who, well, who brought us out west. And these are Hank and Sam, the wagon train guards." She nodded toward the other two men, noticing as they nodded back that their heads were bandaged and they looked as roughed up as Jerome.

Clara was quick to respond. "You mean he's the wagon master that abandoned you and left your brother to die at the hands o' them west-end varmints?" Her eyes narrowed and she looked as though she might just assail Jerome single handedly in spite of her age and stature.

Stella put her arm around Clara's frail shoulders and firmly led her a short distance away. "Children, please come over here. Let Jennifer alone for a bit, please, she' trying to have a conversation and we are not helping her!"

Jennifer smiled thankfully at Stella, and then looked back at Jerome apologetically. "Don't mind Clara. She's a bit outspoken and loud because she's hard of hearing." Jerome nodded, but she could see a certain sense of agony in his face.

For a moment he stared down at his boots and then he looked up and said remorsefully, "I heard about what happened to Russ, Jen, and I want you to know that I am terribly sorry. If I'd had any notion they would go so far as to kill 'im…"

It suddenly dawned on Jennifer that Jerome, along with

most of the people in town, believed Russell to be dead. She considered for a moment that it served him right to keep on believing that for having abandoned them in the first place. Feeling a twinge of conscience at the very thought, she spoke almost in a whisper. "Jerome, Russell got roughed up, same as you, but he's not dead. He's getting stronger every day, and Doc says he'll be just fine." She raised a finger to her lips quickly in a gesture to let him know it was a secret.

Jerome glanced around at everyone and then replied very quietly, "But I heard you had a funeral and all." He stared at her in bewilderment.

She smiled and spoke again in a near whisper, "We put rocks in the casket. Buried 'em." She was glad she hadn't chosen to be vindictive when she saw the genuine relief replace the anguish on his face.

"Jen, I am so glad. Still, I'm awful sorry... Will you tell him when you see him I never meant him any harm?"

"Of course, I will tell him, but I'm sure he already knows it and he bears you no ill will."

Another thought suddenly occurred to Jerome and quietness was forgotten as he asked, "Why are you here? Are you taking the stagecoach, too? Jenny, are we going to be heading back east together?" The hope in his voice was unmistakable.

Jennifer hesitated only briefly before asking, "You're going back east on the stage?"

"Yes. West-end boys caught up to me and the boys when we were on our way back from dropping off the wagon train folks up north. They stole my wagon after they worked us over." Jerome sighed despondently. "I guess we were lucky they left us with a couple horses. We got this far a few days ago. Doc bandaged us up, and we decided to go back east. This town's just no place to be. Neither is this God forsaken prairie desert!" He paused and studied her face inquisitively before saying, "You know, Jen, Pa always said I could work with him in the accounting firm in Boston. It's done a fair business over the years, and I'm done being wagon master. Just had enough. Life's hard enough on the trail as it is, let alone with the likes of them thievin' varmints. Yep, I'm just done with it." For a moment he stared off into the distance and sighed again. Then he looked back at her with unguarded hope in his eyes and repeated his eager question, "Jen, are you coming back east with me on the stage?"

In that moment Jennifer knew her mind was made up as she averted her eyes from his intense gaze. Looking at the small crowd gathered about on the boardwalk she replied decisively and loud enough for all to hear, "No. I'm staying." As she spoke those words, Kathleen gave her a quick nod and immediately went to sit with Hannah. Jennifer knew Kathleen would explain the sudden change of plans to her, and she hoped the woman could accept it without too much question.

Looking back to Jerome, Jennifer said, "There is a woman who's going back east though, she has family there, and has had a rough time out here. Her name is Hannah. At the moment it looks like Kathleen is talking to her, but before the stagecoach leaves I'll introduce you."

CHAPTER EIGHT

Jennifer smiled as she stooped next to the wire fencing of the sheep pasture. A small lamb had strayed from its mother and was within a few feet of the fence staring at Jennifer with wary curiosity. Jennifer held a clump of long grass through the fence in an attempt to coax him closer. "Come on, little fella, I won't hurt you. You are so cute!" Her mollifying words didn't make the lamb scamper away in fright, but neither did they bring him any closer.

She was outside Stella's house near the barns and waiting for Seth to bring the buggy to take her and the children over to the schoolhouse. Stella and Clara were inside, getting the children ready for their first day of school. Jennifer had placed her books and papers down on the wooden plank porch of the small bunk house and wandered over to look at the sheep while she waited. She had so many things on her mind. It had been several days since she had watched the stagecoach roll away from Wolcott heading east, taking along Jerome and his hired men, and also Hannah and another passenger or two.

Thinking back on that day, she remembered her

conversation with Stella after the coach had departed and most of those who had gathered on the boardwalk had made their way home as well. "Jennifer," Stella had said, "you have done a truly noble deed to let Hannah have the ticket and go back east on the stage."

Jennifer had hesitated only a moment before responding, "Stella, I'm not at all sure it was noble of me. I think I had pretty much made up my mind to let her go instead of me, but I am not really sure I would have gone through with it. That's when I saw Jerome come out of the hotel with the other men. When I realized he was taking the stage back east too, I knew there was no way I'd get on the coach and go back with him – you know what I mean?"

Stella had thought quietly for a moment before asking, "You've forgiven him?"

"Oh, yes, I surely have. But my mom always said that you do have to forgive, but that doesn't always mean you necessarily have to let the one you've forgiven become your best friend in the whole world!"

Stella smiled. "Then why didn't you want to go back east on the stage with Jerome along for the trip?"

"It's really just because of his feelings for me. You know, I told you before that part of the reason he abandoned us in the first place was that I wouldn't marry him. No way I was gonna get on that stage with him and have that between us the whole trip."

"Yes, I can see that would have been awkward."

"So you can see that my motivation wasn't exactly pure for Hannah's sake. My mom always said a deed is only as good as the motivation behind it."

"Your mother was a wise woman. Still, I wouldn't worry about it too much. You wanted to do the right thing for Hannah in spite of your fears about staying here. Maybe God knew you just needed a little boost to go through with it." They both laughed a little before Stella continued, "I'm glad you stayed. I know it isn't easy out here, but we all have come to appreciate you, more than you know. That goes for your brother, too. There is hardly a soul in Wolcott that wouldn't give anything he had to help you both out."

"You all have given us so much, and you have been so kind. I don't know what we would have done without you!"

Now, only a few days later, she was actually about to fulfill her dream of becoming a school teacher. The older woman who had been fulfilling the role of teacher for the town had been in failing health for some time, and Doc had finally told her adamantly that she needed to look to her own needs and get adequate rest, which meant no more teaching.

Although at first Jennifer had felt unsure she was ready, the folks of Wolcott seemed confident in her ability to teach. There were just a few school age children, and with the education Jennifer had acquired back east, they had assured her that she would be a good teacher for them. When she had reacted with less enthusiasm than they thought fitting, they had gathered the books and other teaching materials to give to her as a way to increase her confidence.

It only took a day of skimming through the books and examining the materials for her to gain the courage she needed. Her mother had instilled a love for books in her from her earliest recollection. She loved everything from the hard bound covers to the inspiring words and illustrations. When she spoke to the townspeople again, her lack of confidence had been replaced by a simple sense of knowing she was ready for the challenge.

Now she found herself impatiently excited to get started. *With those books and materials in my hands, I know I can teach. I can help the children learn, and that is an amazing thing after all! Of course, there is the very practical side of this teaching opportunity as well, for it will be a way for me to earn some money while I continue for the time being to live with Stella and help her out running her household.*

Her thoughts were interrupted by the clip clop of horse hooves from behind her. She assumed it was Seth bringing up the buggy, so she ignored it and continued to try to coax the lamb closer. She hoped the clatter of the buggy wouldn't send it scampering back to its mother. After a moment she realized she was hearing just a horse, no buggy, and wondered if perhaps a parent was coming by to say hello to the new teacher. Giving up on the lamb, she stood up and turned around as a man brought his horse to a halt near her.

"Hello," she said with a gracious smile, although she was surprised not to recognize him. In the small town of Wolcott it was difficult for anyone to remain a stranger for long. "Can I help you with something?"

With a friendly and slightly amused smile, the man glanced from Jennifer to the lamb, which had moved back a few steps and was looking at them curiously. "Maybe I can help you. Looks like you're trying to make a new friend." He dismounted from the horse and plucked a few long stems of grass. Then he stooped down by the fence and began coaxing the lamb. "Here, little fella, you hungry?"

Stooping down at the fence next to him, Jennifer smiled and joined in the efforts to bring the lamb closer to the fence before looking back at the man. She had intended to say something, but somehow forgot what it was as he smiled back at her. His eyes were surprisingly blue, and his smile deepened the dimples in his handsome face. Feeling her own cheeks beginning to flush, Jennifer stood up and tried to remember what she had intended to say. "Umm, do you have children starting school this morning?" *Probably a silly question since he's alone.*

He stood up, but before he had a chance to answer, they both turned to the sound of Clara's voice breaking shrilly over the peaceful chirping of birds and the rippling flow of the nearby creek. "You get outa here, you thievin' rascal! I'll drop you dead right where you stand!" In horror, Jennifer saw that Clara was brandishing a shotgun in the air as she hastened toward them. She was dimly aware that the lamb had bleated in fright and scampered back to its mother.

For Jennifer, the next few moments were somewhat confusing. Clara was coming toward Jennifer and the handsome stranger with all the haste her frail legs could muster, waving the shotgun and crying out, "I'll kill you, you no-good varmint!" However, a glance at the man revealed that he appeared a bit more amused than terrified as Jennifer supposed he should have been. Instinctively, she placed herself between him and the hysterical woman. "Clara, whatever in heaven's name are you doing?" she cried out.

"I don't suppose you know if that thing's loaded?" the man asked with a slight chuckle. He stepped out from behind her and placed himself squarely in Clara's path.

Jennifer moved to stand beside him as she replied, "I've never seen her with a gun before, didn't even know there was one in the house!" It suddenly occurred to her to look to see if the man had a gun himself. A quick glance revealed that indeed he did, and she wondered why he did not make a move to remove it from the holster and at least make a show of defense.

The door to Stella's house suddenly burst open again, and Stella ran out after Clara. "Aunt Clara, will you please put that thing down immediately!" she yelled. But before Stella could overtake Clara, the man had taken a few steps forward and reached Clara himself. Jennifer stared, perplexed, as Clara stopped in her tracks and calmly allowed the man to gently disarm her.

"Dear Aunt Clara, it's so nice to see you," the man said with a chuckle as he held up the gun. "Is this thing loaded?"

"Humph!" was her indignant reply. "Course it's loaded! You think I'd try to shoot the west end boys with a gun that ain't loaded?"

Jennifer drew in a sharp breath as she stared at Clara and the stranger in utter disbelief. *West end boys? Surely he can't be one of them!*

Catching up to the group, Stella paused a moment to catch her breath, and then she answered the question. "It's not loaded." She took the gun from the man and checked inside to be sure. Then she asked, "Robert, you're here rather early this morning. Is everything all right?"

The man stopped grinning at Clara, who stood glaring at him with her arms crossed defiantly, and responded soberly, "Stella, can we talk?"

"Of course we can. Aunt Clara, please go sit down on the porch with Jenny." She motioned to the porch where Jennifer's books still lay. "Jenny dear, please keep an eye on her for just a few minutes."

As Stella and the man walked a short distance away, Jennifer sat on the porch with Clara as she sat peacefully catching her breath. "What did you mean, west end boys?"

Jennifer asked her hesitantly, her mind still spinning from the woman's shocking behavior.

Clara scrutinized her for a moment, and then broke into a cackling laugh. "Oh, I see. You think because he has blue eyes and a nice smile he couldn't possibly be one of them! That's it, ain't it?" She laughed and slapped her knees, looked again at the confusion on Jennifer's face and laughed until a tear trickled down her leathery cheek.

When her laughter had subsided, Jennifer asked somewhat defensively, "Well, if he's one of them, why'd Stella go off so nicely and talk to him?"

Clara's tone became a bit gruff as she quickly replied, "Because he's her cousin, that's why!" She softened her voice and added with a shrug, "He comes fer a chat ever' once in a while."

Jennifer raised her voice in exasperation. "Then why were you gonna shoot him?"

Clara squinted at Jennifer and said emphatically, "Because, cousin or no, he's a west end varmint, make no mistake about that!" Then she relaxed again and said, "Gun wasn't loaded, I knew that. Jest meant to scare 'im off a bit, that's all. Never woulda hurt 'im. He knows it, too." She was silent for a moment, then chuckled again as she studied Jennifer. "Hoo, hoo! I do believe you was smitten by them blue eyes and dimples!"

Jennifer felt her cheeks begin to redden. "No, no, not at all. I just thought we should be kind to strangers, that's all. Thought he might have been a parent, inquiring about the school. Sure didn't see a need for you to be bringin' out a gun!"

"Well, he's no parent! You'll be happy to know he ain't even married!" Clara chortled gleefully.

The sound of the horse drawn buggy drew their attention. Grateful for the interruption, Jennifer said, "Seth's bringing the buggy. Time to get the children out here so he can take us all to school."

Clara looked in the direction of the buggy, and then she fixed her gaze on Jennifer in amusement once again. "That ain't Seth, dearie! Don't you even recognize your own brother?"

Shocked, Jennifer looked first at Clara, then back at the driver of the buggy. Clara was absolutely right, it was Russell. *And exactly why is it Russell when he should still be in hiding at the Doc's house? What on earth is going on around here today?* She shook her head as if to shake loose the tangled web of confusion from her mind. Then she turned her eyes back on Clara. *And however did Clara know – not only that Russell was not dead, but that it would be him bringing up the buggy and not Seth?*

"Oh, don't look at me like that!" Clara scoffed and waved a hand. "I knowed he wasn't dead! Truth is, you didn't act like somebody's whose brother jest been murdered. Not only that, you kept goin' on over to the doc's house, taking meals and all. Jest ain't normal. So, I went over myself ta other day, jest fer a friendly little chat with Doc's missus. We kept havin' a bit more tea, but she can't hold her water like I can! She finally excused herself to go out back, and that's when I got up, bold as could be, and walked right down that hall and knocked real confident like on the door to that back bedroom. Ha! Yer brother sure was surprised when he opened it, likely he thought I was the Doc or the missus. I looked him square in the eye and I asked 'im, 'And jest who might you be?' And he didn't answer right off, then he said,

'You must be Aunt Clara. It's a pleasure to meet you. I'm Russell, Jennifer's brother.' Yep, that's when I knowed fer sure. Nice feller, seems like, yer brother!"

Jennifer sat speechless as Russell drew up the horses. "Whoa, there! Howdy, Miz Clara! Mornin' Jen!" He doffed his hat with a smile that revealed not only friendliness, but a subtle amusement.

"Howdy yerself." Clara beamed, obviously proud of herself for having solved the mystery.

Russell got down from the buggy as Jennifer stood up and walked resolutely around the horse to greet him. Clenching her fists at her sides and glowering, she demanded, "Russell, what in the world is goin' on here? Why in heaven's name ain't you back at the Doc's?"

Russell smiled patiently as he put his hands on her shoulders. "Jenny, now, I know you're a mite puzzled, but I really need you to not make a fuss here, okay?" His eyes pleaded with her to stay calm.

She would not allow her concerns to be ignored, however, and with a quick glance at Stella and her cousin, she quietly insisted, "Russell, it is not safe for you to be out here! Do you know who that man is?"

Russell nodded and replied, "As a matter of fact, I do. Truth is, I've gotten to know him fairly well over the last few days. Jenny, I need you to trust me here. The man may well be a west end boy, but he is your brother in the Lord first, and he means us no harm. In fact, he intends to help us. I and some of the men of Wolcott knew he'd be joining us here this morning. Now see here, we have got ourselves a plan in place, and you have got to go along with it, understand?" The look she returned him showed plainly she did not intend to even try to understand, so he added, "Not only that, but I've mended up pretty good, and it's time to do something about the situation here!" He stood up straighter and patted his ribs as if to show her he was entirely well.

Stella and her cousin were headed back toward them, and Jennifer could see there was no use in arguing. She took a step back as Stella approached saying, "Morning, Russell. It's nice to see you up and around!"

"Thank you, Stella! It sure feels good to get out of the confines of that room at the doc's!" Russell nodded politely at her, and with a friendly grin, shook the stranger's hand. "Morning, Robert! You ready for this?"

Robert nodded and replied, "Let's get it done!"

Jennifer felt helpless and frightened at the way things were suddenly taking shape. Her hope that Stella might back her up in her concern was dashed as Stella placed a comforting arm around her, but then said, "Don't you boys worry none, we'll be just fine. I'm heading over to the school with the children and Jennifer. Seth will be with us, and Aunt Clara, if she's of a mind to spend the day with us. And look, here come Ben and the other men now, and there's surely safety in numbers. We will be in prayer for you all today, and keep watch for your safe return."

All eyes turned toward the town center. Several men on horseback were heading their way, one of whom led a saddled horse with no rider. It quickly became evident that the horse was for Russell, and Jennifer could only watch as he mounted the horse and rode away with the men, including Stella's husband and her cousin, that handsome stranger who also happened to be one of the west end boys. Russell was determined to go through with 'the plan,' whatever that meant, and she would have to teach school on this, her first day as a teacher, with his safety on her mind above all else. Her stomach began to tie up in knots, but she knew there really was nothing she could do, except, as Stella had said, to pray.

CHAPTER NINE

When Seth and the older girls came out of the house bringing the little ones, Jennifer could see that the girls had been crying. "Mom," Sara Lynn asked Stella in a subdued voice, "Is Father going to be all right?"

Stella hugged her for a moment before replying, "Sweetheart, don't be crying now. We don't want to frighten the little ones. We will pray and trust the Lord for the safe return of Father and all our men folk."

Dorinda crowded in for a hug as well, exclaiming as she did, "I hate those west end boys! I wish things had never turned out the way they have!"

Even as she put her arm around her, Stella was quick to reply, "Dorinda, please don't say 'hate.' I understand your feelings, dear, but we must remember to pray, even for those who are our enemies."

"I know Mom, but I'm scared."

"I know dear, we all are, but we have to be brave, for the

children. The Lord will see us through this, Dorinda, you must trust Him."

It occurred to Jennifer that she also would need to be brave so as not to frighten the young children. *I don't feel brave. But what can I do? As Stella just said, trust Him.* Still, she couldn't help but sighing disconsolately, and for a fleeting moment she wished that Russell had not yet healed up well enough to ride with the group of men. Mechanically, she took Stevie from Seth so that he could help everyone into the buggy. Then, when Sara Lynn was seated, she put Stevie on her lap and gathered up the books she'd left on the porch. It was a bit crowded, but shortly they were all in the buggy, heading for the schoolhouse.

When they arrived and everyone had gotten out of the buggy, Jennifer watched as Seth reached into a compartment in the back of the buggy and removed the shotgun Clara had been waving in the air just a short time earlier. When he withdrew shells from a pocket, she realized that the young man had the responsibility of protecting the women and children on this day as no one really knew for sure what might happen. In spite of his youthfully shy behavior, she knew that he was also both mature and brave for his young age of seventeen. She prayed silently that nothing would happen that day that would require him to have to use the shotgun.

Children were beginning to arrive for school, most accompanied by their mothers, and none in a hurry to get inside the schoolhouse. They began to run and play together while their mothers gathered into a group and talked in hushed tones. Jennifer was sure they felt a need to comfort and encourage one another as most of their husbands were on the mission with Ben and Russell.

The early morning chill in the air was a sure sign that

winter would soon take the place of the pleasant days of autumn. Although on this first day of school most of the school age children were present, Jennifer knew that most of the older children would not be attending school regularly until the harvest was brought in from the fields. She imagined them striving to get it done before freezing temperatures brought an end to the season, and wondered if they would resent not being in school with the other children. As she looked around, she noticed that the women were not leaving, and she was sure it had more to do with the nature of the business the men were attending to that day than to oversee the students, or perhaps even herself as the new teacher. "Safety in numbers," she whispered to no one in particular. With a glance toward the western end of town, she pulled her shawl tighter around her shoulders and headed toward the schoolhouse door.

Stella pulled out a key and opened the door, calling out, "Come on, children, time for school to begin!" Amid much scuffling of feet and laughter, the children ran into the one-room schoolhouse and began to bicker over who got to sit where on the long benches. Jennifer was glad for the presence of the women, especially Stella, who was not afraid to take charge and get the students settled down.

The classroom was simple. A large teacher's desk was at the front of the room with a large blackboard on the wall behind it. Benches were placed in rows for the students. Shelves lining the wall in the back of the room were for books and school supplies as well as a place to store packed lunches and other student belongings.

Shortly the children were all seated, and Clara and the mothers remained standing or sat on a bench in the back of the room. Seth stood alertly on the shaded porch, the loaded shotgun cradled in the crook of his elbow. Standing at the head of the class, Jennifer took a deep breath and said a bit nervously, "We'll start with prayer. Everyone please bow your heads." She said a simple prayer asking God to bless the day, the school and the students, and then she added, "And dear Lord, please protect the men today as they attempt to bring safety and order to this town."

Next she made a list of names, having each child state his name and age. She would use that to take roll call in the coming days. Then, after handing out slates along with chalk, she picked up a spelling primer from her stack of books and began to read words with their definitions, asking the students to first recite the words in unison and then attempt to spell them out on the slates.

For a while there was only the murmur of classroom recitation, with nothing more than the sound of chirping birds coming from outside. Suddenly though, a shout from Seth broke the early morning calm. "Riders headin' this way!" Orderliness was shattered as everyone ran and crowded at the windows and doorway, trying to see who was coming.

Jennifer knew it was far too early for the men to be returning, so she felt a mild sense of panic as she wondered if the riders had anything to do with the business of the menfolk. "Children, go back to your seats," she scolded.

Stella backed her up quickly with, "Yes, do it now!" She and the other women made sure all the children were back in their seats before returning to the door and windows to see who was riding up.

Seth nodded to let the women know it was okay to come out of the schoolhouse. As they hastened outside, they saw that the riders indeed were not their men folk returning, but a group from the tribe of Indians that lived nearby. Jennifer recognized the one who seemed to be in the lead – it was the very man who had sold the much needed horse to Russell for their wagon. He approached with only one of the other riders, a woman, while his companions halted their horses and waited a short distance away. Recognizing Jennifer and many of the others, the man raised his hand in a greeting of peace before dismounting and motioning for the woman to do likewise. He smiled and nodded at the women as he approached, but stopped to stand before Jennifer, motioning again for the woman to follow. "Good day," he greeted Jennifer. "Your brother, he is well now?"

"Yes, thank you, he is very much better."

With a wave of his arm toward the still-mounted group, he announced, "We will go, find brother and help him."

Jennifer was momentarily confused. Apparently, the Indians had known about the plan for this day. Even Clara, who was not ever supposed to be told much of anything, had known. Everybody, it seemed, already knew about today but her. Quickly dismissing a twinge of resentment about that, she exclaimed, "Yes! Thank you so much for helping our men folk."

Stella was quick to voice agreement. "Yes, that would be good! Our men need all the help they can get today!"

The man nodded yet remained standing with the young Indian woman beside him, an unspoken question in his eyes. Perhaps he wanted to leave the woman with the town women for safety, so Jennifer asked, "Is there something we can do perhaps to help you?"

"You teach. You teach English. You read Bible and teach English to wife?"

Jennifer remembered reading the scriptures to the Indian

man on first meeting him, and how surprised she had been to realize that he knew Jesus. She looked now at the lovely face of his wife, with her guileless but apprehensive brown eyes, and smiled reassuringly. "Yes, of course. I will teach English to your wife. She can sit with us today and learn English. We will read the Bible."

After a few nods and parting greetings, the men of the tribe rode toward the western end of town, and shortly the women were back inside the schoolhouse and the lessons continued. Spelling was followed by some basic arithmetic with Jennifer writing a simple problem on the blackboard, and the students copying the problem onto their slates and then attempting to fill in the answer. After a while she invited the older children to help the younger ones with simple arithmetic and spelling words. She had been assured by Stella that it would help reinforce the learning of the older students to help the younger ones in this way, and it would also allow her time with any students that needed individual attention, as well as time to prepare lessons. On this unusual day it also gave her some time to spend with the Indian man's wife. The woman was attentive and learned quickly, although Jennifer realized it was partly because she had already been taught some of the English language.

The day went by quickly. Jennifer was glad to have the extra help, not only of the older children, but of the mothers and even Clara, who particularly enjoyed helping the youngest of the children learn to draw the letters and numbers on their slate boards. The few babies in the group were alternately being held and fed, or playing and napping on blankets spread on the floor. A lunch break was called, and then the students were given a few minutes to play outside under the watchful eyes of Seth and the mothers before being brought back in to resume their lessons. It was midafternoon before Seth once again called out, "Riders headin' this way!"

As before, the women restrained the children with admonishments to get back to their seats and then hastened outside. Most of the riders, both the men folk of the town and the Indian group, were coming toward the schoolhouse, but a few were hurrying toward the house of the town doctor. The reason for their urgency to see Doc was quickly evident – one man was not riding a horse, but was being brought along in a buckboard. Jennifer's heart sank and she prayed silently. *Oh no! Please, Lord, don't let it be Russell again!*

Jennifer was on her way to the Doc's house carrying a basket filled with freshly baked bread and beef stew. As she walked she thought back on all the events that had led up to this day. So much had happened since she and Russell had left home to find their dreams by going out west with the wagon train. It seemed like it had been such a long time ago, but really it had only been a few months.

As she walked, she wondered what their dear mother would have thought if she could see them now. Russell had always been so strong in his faith, just like their mother. But Jennifer knew she had also grown in both faith and maturity since the beginning of their journey. An attitude of thankfulness had settled in her heart, and a confidence that whatever might happen, God would indeed see them through it all. In thankfulness she prayed quietly, "Thank you, God, for all You have brought us through. Even when I was stubborn and fearful, and sometimes I wasn't even sure You were there, You were faithful and patient! And You surely have delivered not only Russell and me, but this whole town from a terrible situation."

Her thoughts turned to what Russell had told her of the frightening day the men of Wolcott, with help from men of the Indian tribe, had gone to the west end ranch to rid it of the outlaws and their dreadful domination over the town. The Indians had caught up to them before they had gotten all the way to the ranch. Then they had split into two groups, the smaller of the two groups riding in on the main road, but the larger going in from the back where they were less likely to be seen because of the cover of rocky hills, trees and brushwood.

"You know, Jen," Russell had said, "I'm not at all sure we would have been successful without the help of the Indians! Robert walked right in the front door, calm as could be, with the Indians sneaking in quietly right behind him. You should have seen those west end boys running out the back doors! They were so surprised they didn't even have time to grab a gun. After that it didn't take much for us to get 'em all rounded up. But then we were doin' a headcount, and Robert told us for sure someone was missing. We were headin' for the cellar to have a look when the door to it opened up a crack, and out popped the barrel of a shotgun! We didn't have much time to react, that's for sure! Well, you know how that turned out. Good thing is they are all in jail now with guards and waiting for trial. We're certain after the trial they will receive a cavalry escort to prison!"

Now as she walked, Jennifer prayed silently that all would go according to God's plan where the trial was concerned. Although the town surely had some sense of security now that the troublesome circumstances seemed to be over, there were still things to consider.

A voice from behind her suddenly broke into her reverie. "Hey, Sis, let me help you with that." Russell caught up to her from behind and took the basket. "Gosh, you don't bring me bread and stew anymore!"

"You don't need it brought to you; you can set up to the table just like the rest of us. And don't you think I don't thank the Lord for that every single day!"

"Yeah, the Lord sure has been good to us! Still, this sure does smell tempting. You think he'd notice if a bite or two was missing?"

Jennifer jabbed Russell's ribs. "Don't you touch it! It's not for you! Besides, there's plenty more back at Stella's."

"Yeah, I know. Just thought it might taste better bein' his, you know!"

"Hmmm. Well, I really hope he enjoys it. Do you think he truly is mending up all right? Doc said so yesterday, but you know he's been in that bed for more'n two weeks now!"

Russell patted his chest and asked in a lightly mocking tone, "Do I detect deep-hearted concern?"

Blushing, Jennifer replied, "Well, Robert is Stella's cousin, you know, and he did so much to help out the whole town, you know, getting rid of the west end boys in spite of his being one of them. Don't you think it's right to be concerned for his health? And bringing him a bite to eat doesn't seem like much to do for him, compared to everything he's done to help us!"

"Oh, yes, of course, that's what this is all about," Russell replied teasingly. "Couldn't be because of them blue eyes and dimples Clara says you been smitten by!"

"Oh Russell, for pity's sake! You do know better than to listen to the musings of an elderly woman, don't you?"

Russell laughed, then he was quiet for a moment before he said soberly, "You know, Jen, he seems to think there's a chance you'll marry him."

Jennifer stopped in her tracks and stared at her brother. Turning to face her, Russell said once again in a lightly mocking voice, "Don't worry, I told him flat you'd not likely do any such thing!"

Her eyes grew even wider as she asked, "You told him that?"

Russell laughed heartily, and then said affectionately, "Jen, what I really told him is that I thought he might actually have a chance at marryin' you! He seemed pleased."

Jennifer sighed in relief. "Oh. I see." Willing her feet to resume walking, she said, "Well, we'd best get on over there. The stew is getting cold!"

CHAPTER TEN

Jennifer, Kathleen and Stella were sitting at Stella's kitchen table, enjoying a cup of tea. Ben, Russell and Robert had gone out to the west end ranch to meet with Judge Carter and many of the other men of the town. Now that the tyranny was over, the people of the town were anxious to reclaim any of their belongings that they could, and to gain some indication of possible future settlement for the losses the entire town had incurred. At the moment, Jennifer and her friends were content just to share a cup of tea and a peaceful conversation.

Jennifer had been mulling something over. During a lull in the conversation, she finally decided to speak her thoughts. "I'm spoiled." Her flat announcement was met with a moment of silent surprise followed by laughter from both Kathleen and Stella.

"Spoiled! Child, whatever do you mean?" Kathleen looked at Jennifer with an affectionate smile as she asked for clarification.

"Well, it's just that it's something I've known for some

time about myself, but I don't think I've ever really admitted it to anyone," Jennifer replied. "It's a little embarrassing somehow to just blurt it right out loud like that."

"You know you can share whatever is on your heart with us," Kathleen said reassuringly. "We are your friends and we will keep your secrets!"

"Of course," Stella agreed. "But why do you think you are spoiled?"

"It's because of my family. You see, I don't remember my daddy very much because he died when I was very young. But what I do remember about him is that he doted on me, I was his precious little lamb, and he was stern sometimes, but mostly he just loved me! I remember little things, like sitting on his lap while he read to me, and he cut my sandwich just the way I liked it, and he sat me on the horse and led it around very carefully so I could ride like a big person. He made me feel special, not ever like I was a nuisance or something."

"He sounds like a very good father," Stella said. "And we already feel like we know your mother, you have shared so much about her."

"Yes, she doted on me too, although she was strict in ways that she had to be, even more than Daddy had ever been, especially as the years went on after he passed away. But I always knew it was because she loved me very much, and she wanted me to be safe and grow up well. And then there was Russell. You know he's a few years older than me, and he always watched out for me, especially after Daddy died. But he let me play with him and his friends, not like so many older brothers who just tell their younger siblings to go play somewhere else, you know? He treated me like a sister that he cared about, and he also treated me like a parent would, you know, because he felt responsible for both Mom and me. He always took care of us the very best he could."

"You have had a wonderful upbringing, and Russell has done very well being both a brother and like a parent to you," Stella said. "Even we can tell that much from the few months we have known you both."

Jennifer nodded and went on, "He was very protective when we were young. One time I remember Jerome teasing me as he often did. It wasn't malicious, I know he was just trying to get my attention because he liked me, but he went too far and twisted my arm too hard, and when I started to cry he called me a crybaby. And even though Jerome was bigger than Russell, that's when Russell jumped in and really walloped him good! Jerome was a lot more careful how he treated me after that."

Stella smiled and said, "Jenny, you were sheltered by your family because they loved you. Such a blessing, really! A lot of children growing up in this world simply don't have it so good."

Jennifer nodded in agreement. "I had a very best friend growing up, but her life wasn't like mine. Her dad was never home much, she said it was because he was too busy drinking at the bars to bother with home, and her mom had younger kids to take care of, so my friend seemed to be ignored a lot. She pretty much did whatever she pleased because nobody seemed to care what she did. Once when I went to her house, her mom yelled something at her about cleaning her room before she left the house, and she just yelled right back at her that if she wanted it clean she should do it herself, and then we left, and she slammed the door behind us. I couldn't imagine behaving that way toward my mother! I guess she saw the sort of shocked look on my face, but she laughed it off and away we went, down to the corner store to buy penny candy. We liked to sit on the bench outside the store and talk, you know, girl stuff – what boys we liked and all that.

"As we got older, though, I kind of had to stop hanging out with her for a while because, well, you know, she wasn't raised to be a Christian, and the older she got, the more she rebelled and got into trouble. Mom knew, and discouraged the friendship. But then an amazing thing happened. She started going to church with me, and we both joined the choir and sang on Sunday mornings. At first I could tell that for her, the weekly choir practice was just another way to get out of the house at night, but eventually she started asking me questions about Jesus and God. I wasn't really all that strong in faith, but I did believe, and I think over time she really did have faith and believe in the Lord herself."

"That's wonderful for your friend. Life likely would have continued to be very hard for her without your help to find the Lord. Still, I'm not sure why you are thinking about all these things right now?" Kathleen looked puzzled.

Stella looked at her questioningly as well. "I have to agree, we are wondering exactly what is bothering you about all this now."

"It's just that somehow I knew my family pampered me. And maybe in a way I grew up thinking it was deserved or something. It isn't that I regret having been raised by a family that loved me, but somehow it did affect the way I treated people. It was like I always had to be the center of attention, and get my way, or I would often pout. I hate to admit that, really, but it's the truth. Now when I think about my friend Caroline, I often wonder why she put up with me so unwaveringly. She seemed to accept my selfish behavior as if it were normal."

"Maybe it's more that she was willing to accept your behavior because she needed a friend," Kathleen suggested.

"Yes, I think you are right. But it bothers me that I was so self-centered. I shouldn't have treated her that way. And I shouldn't have sulked the way I sometimes did when Mom asked for help with simple chores. I've often treated Russell with less respect than I should have, being bossy toward him and then pouting if he didn't give in. You know, I was fearful about the way things were here, and really didn't think staying here was the right thing to do. But the truth also is that part of the reason I was ready to get on that stagecoach and go back east without Russ was he wouldn't listen and give in to my way of thinking about the way things were. I could see that he was being brave and not ready to give up on our dreams, but I was resentful at least partly just because I wasn't getting my way."

"So," Stella said slowly, "you are feeling guilty about the past. You know the scriptures never vary about the answer to that. 'If we confess our sins He is faithful and righteous to forgive us our sins and to cleanse us from all unrighteousness.' I believe that's found in 1 John."

"I know, and yes, I have confessed the selfishness and my tendency to get resentful, so it's not that I wonder if God has forgiven me. It's more that I'm afraid I might continue to fail in this way."

"Might? Oh honey, we all continue to fail!" Kathleen laughed heartily before calming down and saying more thoughtfully, "Yes indeed, that is exactly why we are so very thankful for God's grace and mercy!"

Jennifer smiled. "Yes, I know. I feel that way too. God is faithful and patient and forgiving. But what I really mean is…" She hesitated before she finally blurted out, "What if after Robert and I are married, I start in treating him like that – you know, bossy and spoiled, and expecting him to just do whatever it is that I want? What if he decides he doesn't love me after all, and maybe goes off to be a trapper in the mountains like Russell intends to do? You know, Russ has already told Robert that I can be a handful sometimes. What if he decides being alone is better than being with me?"

"Oh, now we see, now the truth comes out!" Stella said as she and Kathleen exchanged a knowing look before they burst out laughing.

Kathleen dabbed the tears that the laughter was starting to bring, and then she said, "Honey, don't mind us for laughing a bit. We know your feelings and concerns are very real and we do not mean to laugh them off. The truth is that Stella and I have both had very similar concerns with our own husbands. Jennifer, every Christian woman who ever marries has similar feelings and concerns! It's true that the Bible does say that women are to respect their husbands, but remember that it also does say the men are to love their wives. There is a very healthy balance, and the couple that finds that balance is truly blessed!"

Stella agreed, "Yes, but it doesn't always feel balanced, and sometimes it will seem quite unfair. You will learn to trust God and seek His strength diligently to keep on being faithful and respectful even when you feel Robert may not deserve it. And there will be times he will have to persevere as well, making a deliberate choice to love you even when you do fail and behave disrespectfully, or as you say, in a spoiled or selfish manner. But Jen, it's easy to see that he loves you. And I think it's safe to say he will be with you long past the honeymoon! He's strong in his faith, and although you will both experience the challenges of marriage, I am confident he will – no, you both will – do what you must to have a lasting and happy marriage."

Jennifer sighed. "I hope so. But sometimes marriage sounds like a lot of work!"

"It most certainly is a lot of work!" Kathleen said. "But you must remember that it's also one of God's greatest blessings!"

Suddenly the sound of horses outside and then the thudding of boots on the porch interrupted the conversation. The women smiled understandingly at each other. The men were back, and finishing the conversation would have to wait.

"Well, it's official," Ben announced to the women as he came into the kitchen with Russell and Robert. "Judge Carter has released from evidence a lot of the property that may have belonged to the town folk. He feels they don't need to keep every single article in evidence for trial. We'll be heading over there in the morning, and we'd be obliged if you women folk would come along. We stopped by Clara's house on the way back, and she insists she wants to come along, says she hopes to find a music box that came up missin' a while back. It don't sound like the sort of thing the west end boys would have taken, but who am I to say? Anyways, she'll be a headin' over here in the morning so she can go along with us."

Stella smiled as she answered her husband. "Likely she is mostly just curious and wants to come along for the adventure. You know how she can be, never wanting to be left out of anything!" She stood up and stared for a moment at the star shaped badge on Ben's shirt. "You know it's going to take me a while to get used to seeing that – again." She patted the badge and gave him a quick kiss on the cheek.

Jennifer knew it was difficult for Stella to accept once again that it was her own husband in the dangerous job of protecting the territory, just as it had been years ago for her father. She silently said a prayer for Ben's protection, as well as for the men who had agreed to be deputies.

Her thoughts turned quickly from Ben, however, to another man in the room. She smiled shyly at Robert as their eyes met briefly. She wondered if again tonight they would sit alone together on Stella's front porch in the rocking chairs, talking late into the evening until Ben came out on the porch to invite Robert to go home and come back the following day.

Later that evening, Jennifer and Robert did sit out on the porch. They had been chatting casually, and somewhat intermittently, both enjoying the cool evening and the simple pleasure of spending time together. Jennifer, however, had something on her mind, and after a while she hesitantly brought it up. "You know, Robert, I don't mean to pry, but I have been wondering something."

"Ask away, I'm not shy!"

Jennifer smiled. Indeed he was not shy. But she was a bit, and at times she found it difficult to begin a conversation with him. Like now. Still, there were things she wanted to understand, especially if they were going to be married. "It's just that, well, you grew up on the west end ranch along with your brothers. Yet you turned out so completely different. Can you help me to understand how you managed to do that?"

He smiled and reached out to touch a curl of her hair. "I can see how that might be confusing. The fact is if not for

Uncle Samuel and Stella, I probably would have turned out pretty much the same as my brothers. I was the youngest of the bunch, and I guess that also turned out to be somewhat of a help. In their own ways, my brothers tended not to try to drag me into much of what they were doing. Uncle Samuel and Stella and Stella's first husband tried the best they could to get us into church, especially Pa. Pa wouldn't go, nor would my brothers, but one day Pa pointed at me and said, "Take him!" So, they did. I was really young, didn't understand anything at first, but I went more and more often, and one day it all began to make sense. The pastor we had back then gave one more altar call and down that aisle I went. I asked Jesus to forgive me for the bad things I'd done, and the pastor assured me that He forgave anyone who confessed their sins. Stella gave me my first Bible."

He paused for a moment, and Jennifer could see that he was deep in thought. She didn't want to stir any unpleasant memories, and hoped it hadn't been wrong for her to ask about his childhood.

He continued, however. "Even that all might not have made that much difference, but Uncle Samuel and Stella started having me stay with them quite a lot after Mom died. They could see how bad things were getting, and wanted to do whatever they could to head things off for my sake. Well, you know what happened to Uncle Sam and Stella's first husband. But fortunately for me, Ben was the same way after he and Stella were married. He had me stay on here at the ranch for sometimes months on end. I learned everything I know about ranching from him, really. So, they made sure I got to school, and I'd help out on the ranch, and Ben would take me fishing, me and Seth too as he got old enough. And of course we always went to church."

Robert sighed and remained quiet for a while before he went on, "The thing is, what I was learning in church I saw being lived out right in front of me here. But back at the west end, I'd begin to get confused, I suppose. They all didn't want to hear about Jesus, that's for sure. Called me a sissy and other names much less repeatable. I started spending more and more time here. One day I finally just gathered up my stuff, and when Pa saw I was headed out he asked where the hell I was going, so I said I'm going to Ben and Stella's, and he just said good riddance. I think he knew I wouldn't be back much after that. I worked some at the livery in town, even some for Bart, the general store owner, plus Ben here was paying me as a ranch hand and I was staying in the bunk house for a time."

He paused again and smiled at Jennifer. "Am I boring you?"

"No, not at all! I just hope you don't mind – well, telling me things that may be hard to talk about. It's really helpful – you know – I feel so much like I'm finally beginning to understand!"

"I don't mind telling this all to you – I feel like I can talk to you about most anything! Well, after a few years of being back at the ranch only every so often, and nobody seeming to mind if I came or went, I decided to stay out at the west end most of the time the last couple of years or so. I'd grown as a Christian, and somehow I hoped I might make a difference. Not only that, but Pa was getting on in years, and needed a helping hand with things more. Nobody else paying much attention, too busy with drinking and gambling, and, well, you know." Robert's head hung rather low as he made that last statement.

"I know," Jennifer said sympathetically. "It's okay, you don't have to say more, I really do understand now." She placed her hand on top of his as she spoke.

He lifted her hand and kissed it before saying, "I want to finish. I may never talk like this again, but it's important to me that you understand everything before we marry."

"Okay," she said with a nod.

"Things were just going from bad to worse, and after a lot of prayer and agonizing over the situation, I finally came to the conclusion that everybody – the town folk and my brothers and Pa too – would be better off if the lot of 'em were in jail. I'd been in on the meetings with the men from town, and I finally agreed to help them try to get Pa and my brothers into custody. By far the most difficult decision I've ever had to make. But now that it has finally happened, just like everyone else in this town I have a huge sense of relief and peace. I am at the same time grieved, but I want you to know that I also do have hope for my family. I intend to try to visit them in prison, and to take things to them, whatever they need, and to pray for opportunities to tell them about Jesus, how He still loves them and will forgive them if they will just pray and ask Him to. Or, if they still won't listen to me, I'm praying that God will send them someone they will listen to."

Just then Ben came out onto the porch and made polite conversation for a few minutes before saying, "Well, you know it's getting pretty late. We have to get to the west end ranch – go through some stuff – and work around here as usual, so we'll likely be getting an early start in the morning." He yawned and stretched.

Jennifer felt the evening had come to an end all too soon. But they recognized their cue, and smiled a bit sadly at each other as Ben went back into the house. Then they stood, kissed lightly and said goodnight.

The next morning at the west end ranch, Jennifer was in one of the back bedrooms, kneeling over the open trunk of their family keepsakes, removing items and setting them aside on the floor. She didn't notice Robert standing in the doorway watching her until he spoke.

"I'm sorry," he said. "I tried to get them to leave the trunk alone, but they wouldn't listen to me."

Jennifer looked up and gave him a quick smile, then she went back to taking things out of the trunk. She hardly noticed the pieces of broken china and wrinkled table linens as she set them aside. At last she reached what she most wanted to see – her mother's wedding dress wrapped in paper. She blinked back the tears. "My mother's dress," she practically whispered. "I thought I would never see it again!" She carefully removed the rumpled paper, and then she stood up and held out the dress so she could look at it. "Isn't it beautiful? My mother was beautiful. I miss her so much."

"I tried to fold it back up and wrap it up in the paper again the best I could," Robert said quietly.

Jennifer quickly wiped away the tears that were beginning to spill over as she looked at Robert with a playful smile. Holding the dress to her shoulder and waist, she began to dance slowly about the room, twirling the long lacy skirt.

Robert smiled as he watched her. He started to say something, but just then Russell joined him in the doorway.

"Jenny, what are you doing?" Russell asked with a chuckle. "You know the man you marry isn't supposed to see you in the dress before your wedding day!"

"Who says he is? I'm not actually in the dress; it's just draped in front of me!" Jennifer laughed mischievously and then she continued to twirl.

'*My* dear Caroline,' Jennifer wrote on her stationery, 'I apologize for not writing to you sooner, although as you might expect, it would have been difficult to get a letter to you as we traveled out here. First I would like to ask about you. How are you? And what has happened since we parted? I hope we can begin to write often.

'I have so many things to tell you that I hardly know where to begin. I suppose that I should begin at the beginning and tell you of the journey, how it started out as a most remarkable and exciting adventure, but soon became increasingly difficult, and then, but for God, it truly became quite impossible. I have learned something very important, though, and that is that God can be trusted in even the most difficult of situations. But instead of explaining all that now, I think I will tell you first what has my heart so full at this time that I can very nearly think of nothing else, and that is that I am to be married. I am sure you would approve of my beloved Robert, he has blue eyes and dimples, and he simply is extraordinary in every way. I know now that I have never truly been in love before.'